A Time of Our Own

Adam Rhodes

Cover by Anna Chamberlain

Contents

Family First	5
Halloween Stories	11
Ancient Dark	15
Dear, Sweet Jane	43
A Time of Our Own	49
Slap	81
The Drifting Wars	86
Beware the Fae	111
The Ones that Crawl Out are Fat and Stout	133
The Tree	136

Family First

The first drop of water slammed onto the car's windscreen, just as the engine powered down. Flinging open the car door, Ewan raced towards the house, remembering his coat was still on the chair in his kitchen.
As he ran towards the house and drops of rain started to hit the ground around him, the door opened. Ewan barged his way in, seconds before the heavy rain thudded on the ground, soaking it in seconds.
Ewan stopped to breathe for a moment, taking pride in his speed and his near-miss. He was violently knocked onto his back and something started to rummage through his pockets, digging deep and not letting him stand up.
'Laura! Tommy! Get off your uncle!'

The twins stopped their desperate search for sweets, allowing their uncle to climb to his feet. Rachel, who had scolded the children, stood in the kitchen doorway, wearing a small apron, with a ladle in her hand. She walked over and hugged Ewan, pulling him in close and whispering him a welcome, before turning and returning to the kitchen.
As she disappeared from sight, Ewan pulled a couple of small lollipops out from his blazer pocket and gave them to the six-year-olds, who did the usual fingers to lips silence sign, to protect their forbidden treasures. Ewan smiled and walked into the living room, the warmth and dry of the house a stark contrast to the

pouring rain outside.

Freddie was sitting on the sofa, headphones in and his face was buried in a small book. Opposite him, Marie sat, sketching on a large pad.
She looked up and smiled as she saw Ewan, getting up to hug him.
'Uncle Ewan, I missed you!' She said, with a small laugh. She was tall for a fourteen-year-old.
'I missed you too.' Ewan replied, before turning his head. 'Hey Freddo.'
Freddie looked up, gave a small wave and then returned to his book.
Continuing his journey through the house, passing the dining room, Ewan entered the kitchen. Rachel was stirring a large pot with the ladle she held earlier, while Ken, her husband, chopped up several vegetables with a large knife.
Seeing Ewan, he stopped focusing on the onion he was dicing and outstretched a slightly slimy hand. Ewan took it hesitantly and then accepted the beer offer that followed.
'Dinner will be ready soon, Ewan. Go and have a sit-down. You've had a long drive.' Ken said.
'Thanks, it's great to see you all again.' Ewan replied, with a smile, sipping on his beer.
He wandered into the living room again and sat on the soft armchair, facing both Freddie and Marie.
It was a few minutes before the rain ceased and the sun began to shine through the breaking clouds.
'Finally some actual summer sunshine.' Marie said, looking up from her sketchbook.
'It won't last long. We live in England, it always rains

here.' Freddie responded, as positive as ever.

Rachel and Ken walked in, followed by the squabbling twins, placing several bowls of vegetables, potatoes and salad on the table. Ken returned to the kitchen momentarily, before walking out once again carrying a large casserole dish.
'Dinner is ready!' the twins shouted, almost in unison.
Marie, Freddie and Ewan all made their way to the table and sat down. Everyone began to dish out the food onto their plates and began to eat.
Rachel was the first to speak and break the silence of eating.
'So Ewan, how is work going?'
He swallowed his mouthful and wiped his mouth with a napkin.
'Yeah, it's alright. I mean, working in an office day to day is a bit different to being a missionary, but you get used to it. It's far less demanding and there are far fewer confessions.' He said with a laugh. Everyone else laughed, including the young twins, but only because of mob mentality.
'I'm happier now. I would rather be an accountant in a warm office than outside in that.' Ewan pointed out of the window.
'Got to go outside sometimes though bro.' Ken said with a mouthful.
Marie finished her mouthful of carrots and spooned more onto her plate.
'How is Danielle?' She asked.
'She is well, thank you. She apologises she couldn't be with us tonight, but she had to work late. She says being a doctor in ER is rewarding, but the workload is

more often than not, overbearing.' Ewan said, using his knife to push food onto his fork.

'Freddie, Marie, school going well?' He asked just before he put the food in his mouth.

Freddie gave his usual grunt of a reply, while Marie went into greater detail, which wasn't uncommon.

'Just finished my draft for my GCSE art final, I had a try-out for the hockey team and I am also acting in the school play. The next few weeks are going to be really busy.' She said.

Ewan could tell that even as the young girl said this and ate her meal, she was going over script lines and revisions in her head. Marie rarely knew how to switch off and just relax.

Ewan turned towards the twins.

'What about you two?' he asked.

Laura didn't look up, but instead focused on shovelling peas down her throat, throwing a quick thumbs up towards her uncle.

Tommy hadn't touched any of his food. He was quite pale and was looking towards his feet.

Suddenly the young boy rushed from the table and towards the toilet, the door closing behind him. There was the sound of retching a few moments later.

Rachel sighed and stood up, following her son through the toilet door. From within, her voice softly comforted Tommy.

'Tommy hasn't been very well recently,' Ken said, sipping his beer.

'He has been covered head to toe in a rash. It's made him scratch himself raw. He's also completely off his food.'

'That is very unlike Tommy.' Ewan said, looking

towards the toilet door.
'Weirdly unlike him. We are hoping it will pass soon. The doctor gave us some medicine to help lower his temperature. We are hoping it is just an extreme case of the flu.' Ken said.
Rachel and Tommy remained in the toilet for a short while, so Ken and Ewan cleared the table while the other kids busied themselves by starting the washing up.

Ewan could hear more retching from the toilet, but underneath it, the soft sound of music. The music sounded like it was coming from outside, so Ewan headed to the front door. Looking out into the growing evening, towards his car, he saw that he had left his headlights on.
The music was coming from the radio, muffled by the closed doors.
'Forgot to turn them off when I raced inside.' Ewan muttered to himself with a sigh.
He walked to his car and unlocked it, turning the radio and lights off.
'I hope that hasn't drained my battery too much.' He thought.
Ewan closed the car door and locked it, just as a scream rang out from the house.
He raced back into the house, making sure to pull the door closed behind him.
As he entered the house, he saw Ken and the kids rushing towards the toilet.
Rachel screamed again. Ken put his head in the door and immediately turned, putting himself between Freddie and Marie, shouting at them to go to their

rooms and lock the doors.

Ewan slipped past him and entered the toilet, finding Rachel. She was screaming and crying in the corner of the small room, almost as if she was trying to hide behind the toilet bowl. Tommy was nowhere to be seen, but there was blood, a lot of blood.
The blood was dark and thick, running out of the toilet bowl and onto the floor, pooling around it. Ewan followed the trail of the blood with his eyes. The trail went towards the wall, going up and into the corner of the ceiling, where Tommy hung like a spider.
His hands gripped the walls, his head was twisted backwards and his eyes were a deathly white. Black liquid oozed from his mouth which loosely hung open. Tommy screamed.

Halloween Stories

I sat on the floor, even though there was an empty armchair just behind me. I was to the left of the sofa that Debbie was on and opposite Greg.
Paula and Alex had gone into the kitchen to get some more drinks.
They had been gone about five minutes and it's likely they would now be distracted by each other's bodies. I just hoped they hadn't sullied the kitchen counter, where I prepared my meals.
I stared at the pile of food wrappers in the middle of the room, losing myself in the void that was between a chocolate wrapper and a beer can. Debbie suddenly elbowed me.
'Christ, Gracie, lighten up.' She said.
'Sorry, I think I've had too much to drink.' I replied, rubbing my head.
Alex walked back in carrying a six-pack of beers.
'Gotta get pissed Grace, it's Halloween!' he exclaimed.
Paula followed behind him. Alex's shirt was slightly crumpled and Paula was obviously no longer wearing a bra.
They sat on the floor with me, and a moment later, Debbie joined us, moving from the sofa to the floor.
'In the spirit of All Hallows Eve, who is up for a scary story then?' asked Greg.
Alex made a whooping sound and the girls clapped happily, chanting 'Story, story!'
I just sat there, resting my chin on my knees, trying to get lost into the void again.

Greg scooted forward, pulling out a small torch from his pocket and shined it under his chin, illuminating his face. He looked like an idiot.

'Long ago, on a rainy night, when the moon was full…' Greg began. I yawned.
'The young woman walked slowly back to her apartment after a night out with friends. The only light in the darkness came from the occasional porch, which flicked on as she walked by. Occasionally a car would drive past, the headlamps illuminating the road for a moment.'
Paula giggled and whispered something to Debbie who laughed and playfully hit her, responding with a -
'Oh my god, shut up!'
'She tried to look at her phone to see the time,' Greg continued, 'but the battery had run flat. She wasn't too far from home, but it was cold, dark and silent. Her mind began to wander about the surrounding darkness, so she quickened her pace. She was two streets away from her home when she heard them. The footsteps that grew closer and closer.'
I took a can of beer from the six-pack, opened it and swigged, bored from the poor attempt at horror.
It was a cliché story and I had heard far better.

'The footsteps were slow, but grew loud as they approached.' Greg said. 'Heavy clomps of boots, one after another, closer and closer. The woman dared not to turn around, speeding up her walking pace. No matter how fast she walked, the footsteps never seemed to fall behind, until it sounded like they were right behind her and she broke into a run. As the woman got

to her front door and started fumbling about with her keys, she felt a cold hand touch her shoulder. She screamed!'
At that point, Greg banged the small table to his left. Debbie, Paula and Alex all screamed from the loud and sudden noise.
Seconds later, Alex began to roar with laughter, Greg joining in with him. I just took another sip of my drink, sighing deeply.
Greg took a long swig of his beer and he continued his story.
'The woman spun around but there was no one there. She tried to convince herself it was nothing but the alcohol playing games with her head. She opened her front door and walked into the small apartment. She locked the door behind her and put the catch on, just to be safe. She called out for her little dog, named Patrick, who she could hear moving about in the living room.'
'Patrick?' I interrupted, 'Who names their dog Patrick?'
'Can I continue?' Greg said with a sigh.
'Go ahead.' I said, staring back into my void.

Greg cleared his throat and continued,
'She called out for Patrick once more,' Greg emphasised the dog's name, staring at me in defiance. 'She hoped his presence would calm her. The room was dark and she could see the small dark figure of her dog approach her. She turned on the light, but it wasn't her dog.
The thing was the same size, but instead of legs, it had tentacles and long barbs covered its body. Its eyes were on stalks and its mouth was full of razor-sharp teeth, which dripped with blood. She screamed as it lunged at

her, its jaws opening and tearing into her throat.'
Alex scoffed.
'I thought you were going to make it scary, man. That sucked.' He said.
'It made all of you scream, didn't it?' Greg said in response.
'Sod off, you just made us jump with the table.' Debbie retorted, sticking her middle finger up at Greg.
Greg looked towards me.
'Well, it scared Gracie.' He said.
They all looked at me, but I didn't look back.

I was struck with fear. I couldn't move. The story had faded into white noise because... I could see it. I could see the thing that sat outside the glass door. The thing looking in.
The thing with tentacles and far too many teeth.

Ancient Dark

I stared down the hole, studying the sides, checking for crevices, cracks, even shrubs. Anything that could damage the rope on the descent.
The hole was about three metres wide and descended for about forty, the bottom was partially dark, but the base was just visible with the daylight. There was a sudden temptation to jump, for the thrill of the free fall, but my feet stayed on the ground.
I stepped back, turning back to my truck. I watched as another truck rolled up, kicking up dirt and dust behind it.
James, Peter and Dawn exited once it had stopped and they struggled to pull their bags out with them. I banged the hood of my truck and Mel hopped out to join the group. We all hugged and exchanged greetings, before preparing ourselves for the next step. We chatted as we unpacked.
'New rope?'
'Yeah, bought it yesterday. Nothing special.'
'Got the pickaxes?'
'Fill my bottle for me.'
'Shit, I forgot my pens.'

I fixed my helmet and tightened my belt, pulling on it several times to ensure it would hold. I pulled on the rope from the winch on the front of my truck, clipped it to myself and stood at the edge of the hole and turned on my headlamp. James motioned to me, getting my attention.

'Ella, give us a shout on the walkie-talkie when you hit the bottom.' he said.

'Will do.' With that, I took a step back and descended into the hole.

After a few minutes, my feet hit the ground and I slipped slightly, steadying myself with my left hand, against the side of the hole. I pulled out a glow stick, snapped it and threw it to the ground, the area filling with a green glow. Looking up, I pressed on my walkie-talkie and spoke into it.

'All clear. Come down.'

I watched as the others rappelled down one by one, the silence of the cave being filled with the sound of zipping rope.

Soon, we were all standing on the base ground of the cave, which stretched out from the opening. Circles of torchlight darted around the dark of the cave as it went deeper.

'Right,' James said, 'according to the maps, if we follow this cave, we will come to a small opening and an underground waterfall. There is another cave beyond that point, but as of yet, there is no charted history of it.'

'Why not?' Mel asked, carefully fiddling with the small camcorder she had fixed to her shoulder.

'I don't really know. Most people seem to turn around after the waterfall. Those that have explored further just haven't mapped the course.' James said with a shrug.

'We will be the ones to chart the cave and put it on the map!' He stood like an adventurer. 'Then riches shall be ours!'

'Alright, don't let it go to your head.' I said, trying not to laugh at him.

I took the map he held and quickly scanned it. He was right of course, the map was charted up to the waterfall, but the entrance to the rest of the cave was blocked by red lettering which read 'Area not yet charted.'

We carefully moved through the cave, until it narrowed and it was only large enough for us to get through one person at a time.
Peter, being the largest of us, both in height and girth, went first, just in case. If he could fit in the cave, then all of us could.
Dawn followed him, then Mel, then James and I were last. The cave allowed us to travel standing for a short while until the roof began to slope downwards, forcing us to crouch. We stopped at one section, where we had to crawl on our stomachs. I breathed slowly as I crawled, keeping my eyes on the exit of the tunnel, keeping myself calm. After about three metres, we were able to stand.
We walked a little further, the wet stone closing in around us at times until finally, we came to an open area and the underground waterfall. We stopped and had a drink and some food, sitting on the cold stone ground and took some photos of the waterfall.
There was a period of quiet contemplation that was broken by Mel yelping as some cold water hit her neck.
'Well, this was definitely worth it.' I said to James as we admired the waterfall. He nodded in agreement.
'Hey, look.' Mel said, pointing. The torchlight was dotted on a hole in the side of the cave.
'That must be the uncharted area.' Dawn said, walking towards it and peering in.
'Most likely.' James replied. 'I do wonder why it hasn't

been charted. It isn't like it's hidden or blocked or even difficult to miss.'
'Maybe other people just didn't have enough time to survey the cave?' I said, stepping up to the hole.
'Or they hadn't bought the correct gear. Damn amateurs.' Peter said, finishing off a cereal bar.
'Well, should we do it? For all we know, it could just lead to a dead-end and will be mapped out in five minutes.' Dawn said.
'I say we go for it.' I replied. There was a resounding agreement and we got everything out that we needed. Cameras, compass, tape measure, pens, paper and the map.
After a couple of minutes, we were fully ready and we entered the hole.
We continued forward, with James, being the most experienced caver, leading and with me at the rear of the group once again. This time, we got to stand for a majority of the journey, shuffling sideways through small gaps and occasionally ducking under low ceilings. We stopped once in a while, to take photos, register direction and measure the width and height of the cave system.
We were making good time, with no blockages or dead ends to force us to turn around. Peter, who was in front of me, suddenly stopped. The others kept going, not having noticed.
'Dude, what's up?' I said as Peter's breath started to sharpen.
'I'm...fuck, I'm stuck.' Peter gasped. He struggled for a moment but still didn't move. I put my hand on his shoulder.
'Alright dude, calm down. We have been in this

situation before.' I said. Peter nodded. Being a big guy wasn't exactly ideal for caving.
I moved closer and looked between him and the side of the cave.
'Where do you feel stuck?' I asked.
'My chest. It's lodged I think.' Peter said, using his hand to point.
'Ok, then, like before. When I say, take a deep breath, and then exhale everything.' I said and he nodded quickly.
'Now.'
He breathed in deeply and then released it.
I pushed against him with my entire body weight. This is usually easier with someone else on the other side pulling on Peter's arm.
Peter shifted slightly, stopped and then jolted forward.
'Now keep moving. Don't stop.' I called out behind him. He gave a thumbs up and we kept moving. Trying to catch up with the others. When we did finally catch up with them, it was in another open space.
'How are you guys doing?' I asked, 'we are just dandy.'
There was no reply.
'Guys?'
I looked up, my torch shining on Mel. She held her torch pointed away from her and her face carried a look of astonishment.
I turned to follow her gaze and gasped.
'Bloody hell.'

I pulled out my spare torch and shone it around the area, trying to make sense of what I could see. Dawn had started taking photos with her camera, the flash lighting up the space for a split second.

'So…how the hell has no one surveyed this, let alone reported it?' James said out loud.

'I…have no bloody clue.' I replied.

We stood at the edge of a huge cavern. Directly in front of us, huge man-made stone steps descended towards a large structure that towered in the darkness. It was rectangular at the base, with a cube-like piece in the centre. Tall rectangular towers rose upwards from the base, separate from the central cube. It looked almost like a castle, but unlike any other I had ever seen.

The building was covered in gargoyles, markings in stone and statues of knights and men in robes

I was certain it would have been a spectacle to behold in the light of day.

I pulled out my pad and pencil and drew an extremely quick sketch of the general shape of it.

'Who the hell built this? How old is it?' Dawn uttered.

We stood and stared at the structure, before registering that James had started to descend the steps.

'James, for God's sake be careful.' I called after him.

'I'll be fine. Don't worry.' He called back, waving his hand mindlessly.

Mel sidestepped over to me, not breaking her gaze from the structure.

'I don't like this.' She said. 'It's too weird.'

I agreed with her but said nothing.

I watched as Dawn carefully followed James down the steps, stopping to take photos in all directions, the flash lighting up the dark cavern seconds at a time.

'We need to get closer. Maybe we can even get inside it! This is the discovery of a lifetime!' Peter said gleefully, following the other two down the steps.

I was uneasy about it, but eventually, Mel and I started

to descend the steps as well. James had already reached the bottom and he called up to us.

'There are bones down here! Human bones! A god damn skeleton!'

'Great. Another thing to add to the immense sense of dread that the giant dark castle gives off.' I said to Mel. She breathed out heavily, just as anxious as I was.

'There are more here. But they look different.' James called out again.

'The hell do you mean?' Peter shouted in reply.

'The first lot of bones looked really old. Almost brittle and grey. These ones are different. They look like they have only been here a few days. Still somewhat bloody.' James called out.

'Please, please tell me they belong to a rat.' Dawn said, her voice trembling slightly.

'I don't know. I could only find small bones. They could belong to a wild cat. A fawn maybe.' James said.

I was halfway down the stairs when I stopped and looked around the darkness that clung to the cavern sides.

Mel stood beside me, clasping my hand tightly. There was a loud flapping sound and a strong gust of wind suddenly blew at us.

The air was cold, piercing to the bone and smelt old and stagnant.

'What was that flapping noise?' she asked.

'Bats maybe? They can be common to caves like this. I think.' I said, looking towards the top of the cavern.

I couldn't see anything through the darkness with my torch, so I hoped the bats had flown off somewhere else.

We continued down the stairs, getting closer to the end.

I looked for James' torch, which cut through the darkness, about twenty metres or so from the bottom of the steps. It suddenly went out.

'James? You alright? Did your battery die?' I shouted out. There was no reply, so I pressed the button on the walkie-talkie and repeated my question, to be met with static.

Dawn had reached the bottom of the stairs and she also called out to James, but there was still no reply.

Mel and I hurried down the stairs and carefully made our way towards where we last saw James' light.

At the bottom of the stairs, there was no natural cavern flooring; instead, it was covered by a long strip of stone slabs, edged by pillars. It seemed to stretch from the base of the stairs, all the way to the castle structure for about fifty metres.

It was almost like some kind of fancy bridge.

We carefully walked along it, admiring the craftsmanship of the stone, eventually coming across the bones that James had found.

We hurried to where James had been, only to find no trace of him.

'Where is he?' Mel said. 'Did he go towards the building?'

'I don't think so. I saw his torch go out about here. There is no way he would have tried to walk to the structure in the dark.' I said.

Peter and Dawn came over to us and we spent a few minutes shining our torches in all directions, looking for James.

'What do we do?' Dawn said. 'James has never gone dark on us like this.'

'Maybe he is hiding somewhere. He likes pranks,

right?' Peter said.

James' head and torso dropped in front of us, landing with a sickening crunch and splatter of blood.
We all screamed and Peter turned and vomited. Dawn turned away and fell to her knees, sobbing loudly. Mel immediately ran and held her.
I stared at the mutilated body of my friend, the light from my torch illuminating only a part of him at a time. I felt movement above me and hesitantly, I looked up towards the ceiling of the cave.
I couldn't see through the darkness with just my headlamp, so I slowly raised my torch, until it was shining directly up, where my eyes were looking.
I breathed a release of fear as I saw nothing above us except stone. But surely, that just meant whatever had done this to James had just moved somewhere else.
Suddenly, the ceiling of the cave began to move, almost as if it had suddenly been given life.
As it moved, the sound of scraping stone filled the cavern, catching the attention of the others, who all shined their torches upwards.
As the light illuminated parts of the cavern ceiling, it was clear that there was something there. Something big.
It was large, dark grey in colour and was covered in what looked like fish scales.
The shape was covered in several long spines, many of which were broken. From a central mass, there were long appendages, ending with long hook-like claws, which clung to the stone.
Tattered and torn bat-like wings hung from the appendages and joined the central mass.

From the bottom of the mass swung a long tail-like piece, ending with a partial hook with the point broken off.
Another large mass moved from behind the first.
I shined my torch on it as it moved and watched as a car-sized reptilian head rose up. It stared at me.
The head was covered in broken and missing scales, with a large horn on one side, the other missing, only a small shard remaining.
The mouth slowly opened to reveal hundreds of jagged and broken shark-like teeth. They dripped with blood and the stench was overwhelming.
A single burning red eye stared down at us.

I froze in place. I was unable to move as this thing loomed above me. I am pretty certain I wet myself. Dawn quietly gasped. Mel and Peter remained in stunned silence.
'What…' Peter suddenly uttered.
The creature screamed at us. No roar came from its huge jaws, but a piercing, bone-shattering scream, unlike anything I had ever heard.
'Run!' I shouted and we all bolted, Mel and Peter grabbing Dawn and hauling her to her feet. We ran chaotically through the darkness, our torches flashing around as we didn't take the time to aim them.
There was a large crunching and whoosh sound as the creature let go of the wall and took flight, soaring through the darkness and into silence.
We continued to run, heading towards the large structure in the hope of shelter.
The whooshing sound returned, followed by the piercing scream and a stone pillar to the right of me

exploded in a cloud of dust and debris, peppering my face with tiny pieces.

There was another swooping sound above us and I could feel the air caress my face as the creature flew low, almost within touching distance.
There was a large boom as it landed slightly behind us, kicking up more stone and dirt.
Through the darkness, we were chased by several thundering steps as the creature scrambled after us.
The large structure was now within reach and I lifted my torch to look. Directly in front was a large gate, covered by a huge iron portcullis. Just to the right of it was a small wooden door,
'The door!' I shouted and beelined for it.
I shouldered the wood door, which turned to dust under my weight. I turned and looked out through the doorway, seeing movement in the air behind the others as they ran. Mel ran in through the doorway, followed by Peter, and then Dawn.
There was a thundering crash as the creature's head collided with the structure, its jaws slamming shut.
Dawn fell in through the doorway, screaming and clutching her leg, landing hard on the stone floor.
Her camera went tumbling through the air and landed lense first on the stone floor, breaking apart with undeveloped film spilling out. Peter grabbed Dawn around the waist and pulled her backwards as we ran deep into the building, running blindly into the dark corridors.
There was an almighty boom as the creature crashed against the structure, in what I assumed was an attempt to get at us.

We ran through the rat maze of a building until we stumbled into what seemed like a large hall.
We stayed as quiet as possible for a few moments, trying to catch our breath. An eerie silence descended upon the area. The creature no longer screamed or slammed against the structure. There was just... silence.

'What. The fuck. Was that?' James said between breaths, pointing upwards at nothing in particular.
'I have no idea.' I said, still catching my own breath.
Dawn made a noise and we all suddenly noticed she had gone white as a sheet. Peter helped her lie down on the floor and we examined her.
Her left foot was missing. Her leg ended just after the knee in a horrific mess of shredded skin and muscle. The bone was snapped off, leaving only a jagged point that was split down the centre.
I pulled off a belt and used it to tourniquet Dawns leg. I don't know how much time passed as we worked on her leg, trying to stop the bleeding in the torchlight.
We were forced to cut away parts of Dawn's shredded skin and muscle, in order to stem the bleeding and wrap her leg tightly with bandages. We gave her a belt to bite down on but her screams echoed through the building. The creature screamed in response and the structure shuddered once more. We worked quickly.
We only had a couple of packs of paracetamol and we gave Dawn a couple more than the recommended dose. She managed to get them down and a few moments later, she passed out from the pain, leaving us in silence once the structure had stopped shaking.

***

I drank some water and sat on some steps within the hall, rubbing my face with my hands.
I suddenly vomited, following it with a spit.
Peter walked over to me, shining his torch on my face.
'What the fuck was that?' he said, his voice unnervingly calm.
His voice was calm, but I knew that he was terrified. His eyes gave it away more than anything.
'I don't know.' I said, unable to process everything that had happened within the past two hours.
He sat down next to me.
'Do you think this is why the area had not been surveyed?' He said, drinking some water too.
I considered what he said. How many other people had been down here? How many men and women had met the same fate as James?
'We need to get out of here,' I said, 'If we can get back to the entrance, we can get out.'
'It's a long way to get to through the dark and with that thing on our heels.' Peter said.
'What other options do we really have? We can't stay here. Dawn needs medical attention. She won't last long without it. Even if she did, we'll die of dehydration.'
Dawn stirred on the other side of the room. I got up and walked over to her.
'We should kill it.' She said as I crouched next to her.
'Hey, easy. Rest. You need to save your strength.' I said, taking her hands and gently squeezing them.
That idea was more ludicrous than trying to get out the way we came.

'Mel?' I called out into the dark.

'I'm over here.' I heard her reply. I walked towards her, using my torch to find her in the dark.

She stood alone, looking at a large painting, the face illuminated by the circle of light from her torch.

I walked through the hall and briefly studied it, the light of my torch darting back and forth.

Half a dozen large pillars supported the roof, each with a sconce fixed on them. At one end of the hall, there was a large throne-like seat and what seemed like a fire pit in the centre.

I made my way to the end with the throne. I stared at it, attempting to read the writing that sat under a dust-covered crest on the backrest.

I couldn't understand most of the text underneath the crest, but I could read the word 'Georgius'.

The crest, though dirty, seemed to be a knight sat on a horse, carrying a lance.

I heard Mel call out.

'Guys, you need to see this.'

I gently brushed at the crest with my hand, wiping off the layer of dust and revealing white armour covered with a red cross.

James walked over to Mel and looked at the painting.

'Oh for God's sake.' He said.

The knight's lance pointed down and I followed it with a finger. I wiped away more of the dust that covered the bottom half of the crest.

The lance went down, into the neck of the creature.

I ran over to the painting and stood next to Mel and Peter.

There, in fine brushstrokes of oil paint, was the creature.

Above it, wielding a long lance and clad in ornate armour, was Saint George. In the background of the painting, was a castle similar in structure to the one we currently stood in.
'You are kidding. Please tell me this is an elaborate prank.' Peter said, in an almost annoyed tone.
'That thing is a dragon?'
'There is no way that thing can be a dragon. Dragons aren't bloody real.' Peter said, his anger taking over.
'Technically it's a wyvern.' Mel said.
'Now's not the time Mel.' I said, trying to organise my thoughts.
'Right. Ok. I don't know what to believe right now, but from the circumstantial evidence,' I pointed towards the painting, 'we should probably assume that the thing outside is indeed a dragon.'
'But didn't Saint George kill the dragon?' Peter said.
'In the story, yes he did, after blackmailing the villagers who tried to sacrifice a princess or something. The big flying thing outside says otherwise about being dead. That is, if it is indeed the dragon from the story.'
'It didn't breathe fire.' Mel said.
'Then we are if anything, damn lucky.' I said. 'But, you saw what it did to James and Dawn. We are still in danger and our top priority has got to be getting out of this place and back to town. Then we can warn the authorities and they can do something.'
'How do we get out of here?' Peter said. His anger had subsided and he was now thinking more logically.
'From what you said earlier, we cannot go back the way we came in. It's far too dangerous. The only other option we have is to head further into this place and hope there is an exit somewhere.' I said.

The room was silent for a moment as everyone contemplated the situation.

'Alright,' Mel said. 'Let's get a move on. I want to go home.'

'Peter, can you help Dawn walk?' I asked.

Peter walked over to Dawn and helped her sit up. Mel gave her a hand and got her up on his back, piggyback style. Peter shifted her position a couple of times until he was happy. Dawn held onto Peter, drifting in and out of sleep.

'Right. Ready.' He said.

I walked over to the door that was opposite to the door through which we had entered.

I put my hand on the rust-covered ring handle and turned it. After a moment of resistance, it gave and loudly clunked and I pulled the door open.

There was a sudden, piercing scream.

The entire structure shuddered as the creature struck the side again. We stayed still, staying as silent as possible. After a few moments, no more screams followed.

***

We slowly walked the hallways, guided only by my single headlamp. We all agreed that we needed to save the battery in our torches, so we would take it in turns having them on. We had no idea how long we would be in the structure, and the last thing we needed was to lose our only consistent source of light.

Mel had a small wind-up torch in her bag, but it was our last option, due to it only providing a tiny amount of light. She gave it to me and I placed it in my trouser pocket.

The stale air was silent as we walked, the only sound

being our footsteps on the stone floor.

Mel made a noise and froze in place.

'Something just touched my leg.' She said, her body suddenly paralysed.

I looked down, illuminating the ground. A rat ran past and disappeared into the darkness.

'If there are rats, there must be another entrance.' Peter said.

'It's a possibility,' I said, 'we could try and follow them and they might lead us to an exit. Though, they could just disappear down a crack.'

'Well it's not like we have much else to go on.' said Mel.

We did our best to follow the rats through the darkness but eventually lost them as they scurried down a small drain in the side of the wall.

'Well, shit,' Said Peter. 'So much for that.'

'Wait.' I said. We listened through the silence for a moment. There was a faint sound emanating from somewhere.

'What is it?' Mel asked.

'It sounds like gnawing.' I said, again trying to listen through the following quiet.

'Is it the dragon?' Dawn whispered.

'No, it's not the dragon.' I whispered back. Dawn nodded slowly and passed out again.

I began to walk forward slowly, keeping the light from my headlamp low to the ground.

A few yards in front of us, was a dark mass, low to the floor, in the corner of a turn in the corridor.

I carefully pulled out one of the torches and aimed it at the mass, but didn't turn it on. The gnawing sound seemed to be coming from the mass and it seemed to shift slightly.

I clicked my torch on.

There, crouched in the corner was a man. He stared at us with unnaturally large eyes. He had long and tangled hair, which joined into a long and stained beard.

His arms and chest were near skeletal, covered in a red shirt that was torn and dirty and on his legs, he wore what looked like soiled and ripped jeans.

He held a dead rat in both hands, with a large tear out the side, organs and blood spilling out. Saliva and blood dripped from the man's mouth, from between broken yellow teeth.

He made no noise. He remained sitting in the corner, staring at us. After a few moments of no noise and no movement, I attempted to communicate.

'Hello.' I said, in a whisper. He didn't reply.

'Can you understand me?' I asked. I took a very small step towards him and held my free hand up to show it was empty.

'Can you speak?' I asked. 'Are you hungry? We have food.'

He hadn't moved at all, his eyes open wide and his pupils extremely dilated.

I got next to him and at this point, noticed that he didn't seem to be breathing. I gently touched his hand and felt for his pulse.

'He's dead.' I said with a heavy sigh.

'We just heard him eating.' Mel said. 'He looked right at us.'

'I think,' I said, standing up. 'I think, he died of shock.' I gently moved my hand over his eyes, closing them.

'How long has he been down here?' Peter said.

'Years maybe? I have no idea.' I said.

'All alone in the darkness, with that thing outside. He must have lost his mind.' Mel said, 'It must have been too much for him to see other people again.'

'This isn't a good sign,' I sighed, 'if he is down here still and has been for, I can only assume a long time, then it might mean there isn't a way out.'

'We don't exactly know that.' Peter said. 'We should still check.'

'I agree.' I said. 'But we have to be prepared for any outcome.'

We came to a point where the corridor we were in opened up into a courtyard. I carefully stuck my head out of the arched doorway, looking around slowly and making sure my torchlight didn't rise too high.

From what I could see through the darkness, we were on an upper wall that surrounded the courtyard, which was several feet down on our left.

In the middle of the courtyard sat a large well, and a couple of carts that looked like they were rotting away. On one side, there was a mass of charred wood, which may have been some kind of outhouse.

In the furthest corner, was a large structure that was reminiscent of a large birdcage. On one side, the bars protruded outwards, where whatever was inside had broken free.

'Looks like they tried to keep it in a cage, like a pet.' I whispered to the others.

I slowly stepped out of the doorway, keeping my headlamp down and on the wall. We walked along the length of the wall, crouched as low as possible. We got about halfway along when we stopped.

'Ella, we are far too exposed here. We need to get back inside and find another way.' Peter hissed through the darkness.

'Let's go down into the courtyard.' I whispered. 'There might be some steps down to it.'

I shuffled to the edge of the wall and looked along the sides, spotting some stone steps that descended down. I motioned to the others and slowly led the way.

We took our time to carefully move down the steps, which began to crumble underneath our feet. They held long enough for us to reach the bottom and we hurriedly pressed against the wall in case the moving stone had created too much noise and attracted the creature.

There was silence so we moved again, finding a doorway that was open and led back into the structure.

'I just want to have a quick look around here.' I said to Peter, who chose to remain with Dawn.

Mel and I moved around the courtyard, slowly and carefully. Upon reaching the pile of burnt wood, my torch was able to illuminate scorch marks that covered the wall. It looked like the stone itself had melted slightly.

'Well, maybe the dragon can breathe fire.' Mel whispered.

'Look.' I said quietly, pointing. Carefully, using my torch, moving the light back and forth, we could see bones scattered all around the courtyard.

'Oh my God. There are dozens of bodies here.' Mel whispered.

'The creature probably killed everyone here when it escaped.' I whispered back.

My torch lit up another figure that was sitting against the cage. We slowly moved over to it and saw it was a partial skeleton in plate armour. It was missing the skull and one of the legs.

There was a sword and shield half-buried in the dirt next to it. I brushed the dirt off of the shield and revealed a red cross on a faded white background.

'Do you think it's him?' Mel whispered.

'I have no idea.' I shrugged. 'Maybe. He may have tried to stop the creature when it escaped from the cage and…'

I looked down at the skeleton again and then back at Mel. All I could do was shrug once more. We made our way back to the doorway with Peter and Dawn and made our way inside.

We walked again through the dark corridors of the structure, eventually finding our way into a room that looked like a kitchen. There was a large fire on one side, with a rusted iron spit over it. There were two large and rotted tables that had collapsed under their own weight and there were dozens of rusted pots and pans scattered around the room.

'Well, this seems cosy. We should get some sleep.' I said.

'Thank God, I'm exhausted.' Peter groaned as he carefully shifted Dawn off of his back.

We helped Dawn lie down and then huddled around her, sharing body warmth. I stayed awake for a small while, listening through the silence and eventually, sleep overcame me.

My watch alarm pierced through my sleep and I bolted upright, swearing as I attempted to silence it as the beeping echoed through the empty hallways.

I remained prone, waiting for the piercing scream from the creature, having heard the commotion. Nothing happened and I breathed a huge sigh of relief.

The others were also awake at this time because of my alarm, anxiously looking around for the creature's attacks.

I clicked on my headlamp again, not used to waking up to darkness.

The three of us spent a few minutes changing Dawns bandages, first cleaning her wound as best we could and wrapping it again with the last of the clean bandages we had.

'We need to get out of here soon.' Mel said. 'I think Dawn's wound is starting to get gangrene.'

'Shit.' I said, 'Ok, let's find one today.'

Peter walked over to us.

'Dawn needs the toilet.' he said. The mention of it made me realise that I too needed to go.

'Alright, I'll help her.' Mel said, pulling out a glow stick, getting up and walking over to Dawn. She helped Dawn stand and they entered the corridor nearby. Mel snapped the glow stick and threw it in one of the empty rooms before they followed it.

I found a different room to relieve myself in and then made my way back into the kitchen.

'Peter, Are you almost ready to get moving? Dawn is running out of time really quickly.' I said, standing in the doorway.

'Yeah, sure thing.' Peter said, picking up his bag and slinging it on his back.

There was a deafening scream and the entire wall behind Peter exploded in a cloud of dust and stone and we were both knocked over by the sudden force. Peter landed hard on his front, a few feet away from me. Looking towards the wall, the settling dust unveiled a huge hole, where brick and stone crumbled and fell. As my light shone through the hole, I could see a single large red eye staring through.

There was another scream and another explosion of dust and stone. Peter and I were both covered in the fine stone powder, which I was forced to spit out of my mouth and a large amount of it also found its way into my eyes.

'Peter!' I screamed. The hole was now a lot bigger, with a large portion of the ceiling now missing. Stone and dust blanketed both Peter and a majority of the room.

Peter clambered to his feet, huge piles of dust ran off his body like a waterfall and blood oozed from a wound on his head where he had been struck by a chunk of stone.

The creature screamed and its head descended, jaws clamping around Peter's whole body in one swift movement. There was a whoosh and dust flew into my face again as the creature took to the air, disappearing into the darkness.

I turned and ran into the hallway, telling myself that it wasn't Peter's screams that I could hear in the distance.

'What the hell happened?' Mel asked, holding a glow stick and looking me up and down.

'We have to get going. That way.' I said, pointing down the corridor.

'Where is Peter?' Dawn asked.

I didn't say anything for a moment.

'I'm sorry. He is gone.' I said, putting Dawn's arm over my shoulder and helping her along.

Mel led the way with the glow stick, taking us further into the darkness of the structure.

It didn't take long until we all broke down into tears.

We walked through the corridors for another seemingly long time and came across another room at the top of a long spiral staircase. The room had several rusted swords and spearheads, where the wood of the shaft had rotted away. I assumed it was some kind of guard post. We stopped, putting Dawn down and taking a minute or so to breathe.

I stepped away, brushing the dust off myself and trying to clear my eyes and nose.

'Are you ok?' Mel said, walking over to me.

'Yeah, I'm fine.' I sighed, 'I couldn't do anything to help Peter. He was just…gone.'

Mel rubbed my back affectionately.

'It's alright. You've worked so hard to keep us alive. You've really tried.' She said, softly.

We heard movement behind us.

'Dawn?' I asked, to no reply.

I looked over to where we had placed Dawn down, to see that she had gone.

'Where did she go?' Mel said, at the edge of panic.

'She can't have gone far with her leg.' I said.

We ran out of the room, looking down the only hallway that led away from where we had been. The hallway was short and ended with some more stairs that led up. We raced up them and it didn't take long until we found Dawn. She was surprisingly nimble on the one leg. The stairs opened into one of the four tall towers in the corner of the structure.

Dawn stood on an edge of the tower. Her foot was barely on the edge of the wall. A single shift in weight and she would fall.

'Dawn? For the love of God, what are you doing?' I

said in a hushed voice.

Dawn stayed where she was. I could hear Mel breathing heavily behind me. I slowly moved towards Dawn, hand outstretched.

'Please…step back and come to me.' I said.

Dawn stood silently, staring into the darkness below her.

She smirked and chuckled slightly.

'It's just a bad dream.' she said.

With that, she shifted and was gone.

I screamed and raced to the edge of the tower, looking into the darkness that had consumed Dawn.

The darkness was hypnotising, swirling and pulsing. A white noise that drowned everything out.

I barely noticed the piercing scream or felt the tower shake as the creature landed on one of the corners and peppered me with pieces of stone.

Nothing moved for a few moments and I turned to view the creature. The creature sat on the corner of the tower, its wings folded in and its tail swinging off the edge. It sat, viewing the two of us for what seemed like an extremely long time. Finally, the creature lowered its head to our level, opening its mouth and screamed, displaying its huge shark-esk teeth.

The creature's breath was putrid and I swallowed hard to prevent myself from vomiting. The creature raised its head, preparing to strike. I took my opportunity as it moved away and bolted towards Mel.

I ran into her and essentially shoved her down the stairs.

Seconds after I had taken a few steps down, the entire tower shuddered with a booming crash.

The creature slammed its head into the tower several more times in an attempt to get us. We ran and stumbled and fell down the stairs until we reached a hallway that led away from the tower and we just ran. We only stopped when our legs and lungs begged us to. We spent a few minutes catching our breath, leaning or sitting against the walls. It was at this time that I noticed my face was wet, so I wiped it with my sleeve. A dark substance stained my blue jacket so I pulled a cloth out of my bag and wiped my face with it.

My face was covered in my friend's blood, from when the creature had screamed at me. I quickly wiped it off as best I could and threw the soaked cloth into the darkness.

'What do we do now?' Mel asked, looking at her torch which began to glow dimly. My torch was the same, barely giving any light.

I took Mel by the hand and tried to give her a reassuring smile.

'We walk.' I said. With that, we continued down the dark hallway.

***

It wasn't long until all of our torches had stopped working, so I took out the small wind up torch and used that, the tiny spot of light being the only thing that led us. I wanted to save the last couple of glow sticks until we had absolutely no other choice.

'Hey, is your camera still recording?' I asked, shining my light on Mel's shoulder.

'No,' she said, as I saw the damage, 'I think it smashed a while ago.'

I turned and continued walking down the dark hallway.

'Well, I doubt anyone would believe us about this, even

with video evidence.'

A scream pierced the silence that followed our conversation and the entire structure tremored. There was a crash of stone and the corridor behind us started to cave in.

'Run!' I screamed and we tore down the corridor, followed by the collapsing stone.

The corridor turned twice and the structure shuddered several more times as the creature slammed into it. Luckily, the ceiling stopped collapsing after a few eternal seconds.

We turned one final corner, only to run right into a dead end. We couldn't go back; the hallway was blocked by the collapsed stone.

'Shit! What do we do?' Mel said as I stared at the dead end. I was speechless.

'Oh my god. I don't believe it.' Mel said, pointing.

There, on the wall just left of the dead-end and hiding in the shadows, was a rusty metal ladder. I looked up it using the small torch and from what I could see, it led a long way up.

'Climb it!' I shouted and Mel started to go up it. Moments later, where we were standing exploded into a cloud of dust and rubble as the structure shuddered and the rest of the ceiling collapsed.

We climbed for what seemed like miles, with a rung breaking on us once in a while, teasing a long fall to our deaths. Soon, daylight filled the tunnel. Mel climbed out and I quickly pulled myself out of the hole too. I took a deep breath of clean, fresh air as the bright sunlight blinded me. The tunnel, previously covered by grass and moss, had opened out into a small woodland, where trees gently swayed in the breeze. We sat on the grass-covered ground enjoying the warm sun and the freedom of the outside.

'We escaped.' I said, with a smile and a chuckle.

'I wonder where the hell the trucks are.' Mel said and we had to laugh at the thought.

There was a sudden loud rumble that shook the ground and caused several trees to collapse. The earth close to us began to buckle and crack. We both got up and ran away from the cracking earth, fearing a sinkhole.

There was a final long rumble and the buckled earth burst upwards, like a volcano blowing its top. Dirt, grass, rock and trees were launched far into the air and rained down around us.

Then, there was a scream.

A scream as the creature escaped its former prison.

Dear, Sweet Jane

Alan took his regular deep breath of morning air. He looked towards the rising sun that crested behind the mountains. The light stretched long shadows of trees over his snow-covered lawn and made the ice twinkle. Carefully balancing his cup, briefcase, folders and keys, he stepped through his door and attempted to close it behind him. He managed to do so without dropping anything.

'A good start.' He thought to himself.

He carefully walked down the three steps that lead to his house; getting to his car and realised it was covered in snow. Placing his stuff down on a clear patch of ground, he spent the next few minutes clearing the snow away from the windows while the engine ran, warming the inside.

He grabbed his things, putting them on the backseat and got behind the wheel. The warmth in the car was a welcome escape from the biting cold of the outside world.

After a short drive and one or two small skids on the icy morning roads, Alan arrived at the hospital. He parked his car in one of the designated spots for staff and got out, picking up his things and chugged his coffee, putting the cup back in the holder. He locked the car and made his way into the hospital.

After the short walk and a lift down to the basement of

the hospital, he arrived at the morgue.

Alan waved at Sandra who sat behind the reception desk.

'Good morning!' She said with a broad smile, 'On time for once?' She checked her watch.

'Oops, never mind!'

'Haha, shut up.' Alan said with a laugh. He signed himself in and beeped his ID on the door, letting him in.

Alan entered his office and started to get changed, putting on his scrubs and cap, before washing his hands, giving them a good scrub.

He spent a few minutes looking at the pile of documents on his desk, before walking over to his door and exiting his office.

Simon was walking past and raised his hand in a small wave to Alan.

'Morning, Simon.'

The overweight, middle-aged man slapped Alan on the back and they started walking together.

'Got a fresh one.' Simon said.

'Wonderful,' Alan said, 'what are the details?'

They walked into the operating theatre and walked towards the black body bag that sat on a gurney.

They put on surgical masks and latex gloves and Alan unzipped the bag while Simon read information off the clipboard.

'I knew this moustache was a bad idea. It itches like crazy beneath the mask.' Simon said with a huff.

'It suits you though.' Alan said, not looking up from the body bag.

'Thank you.' Simon replied, with a smile that was hidden by the mask. He looked back to the clipboard.

'Female, Jane Doe, Twenty-four, unknown cause of death.' Simon read.

'Great.' Alan said. 'Always helpful when it's unknown. It's so much easier when you can see the bloody wound with your eyes.'

'Or when the head comes in a separate bag.' Simon said and both men laughed at the morbid joke.

They each took an end and after a count of three, moved the cadaver from the bag to the surgical table. They spent a couple of moments, examining the body, checking for cuts, scrapes and bruises on the skin.

Once they had completed the external check, Simon picked up a scalpel and passed it over to Alan.

'Wait!' Simon said, quickly walking over to the drawer. He pulled out a surgical drape and walked back, placing it over the young woman's body.

'I hate seeing their faces as we cut them open.' He said, shuddering slightly.

Alan laughed and looked down, making the first incision on the chest.

Both men worked quickly and systematically until the chest was open and the ribs were cut. From there, Alan and Simon were able to examine the heart, lungs, stomach and liver.

They then moved further down and examined the

intestines and kidneys.

Finally, they used a circular saw to cut off the top of the skull, to examine the brain.

'We've been at this for hours. There is nothing.' Simon said, taking his gloves off and angrily throwing them in the bin. He stood with his hands on his hips, staring at the cadaver.

'I don't get it.' Alan said. 'The body is fine. This young woman should have been perfectly healthy. There is absolutely nothing external or internal that could be a cause of death.'

Alan spent a few minutes reading through the file that came with the cadaver, before placing it down and walking towards the door.

'Give me a second.' Alan said. 'I'm going to the desk and seeing if they can tell me anything else about where they were found.'

'Get me a coffee would you?' Simon shouted after him, to which Alan gave a thumbs up and turned the corner. He walked down the long hallway which led towards the reception and the crap coffee machine.

After walking to the reception, talking to Sandra and getting absolutely nowhere in regards to gathering more information about the body in the morgue, Alan turned his attention to the coffee machine.

He chose two black coffees, one with sugar. He waited while the machine whirred and popped out the drinks, one styrofoam cup at a time.

Alan returned to the operating theatre, carrying the two cups and placed them both down on the desk by the door.

He blew on his coffee and took a sip, before placing it back down and wandering over to the table.

'Couldn't get any more information from reception.' Alan said, reading off the clipboard again. 'Police found cadaver in a flat at 0954. No sign of forced entry. Possible suicide. Well, we can deny that reasoning. '

Alan looked up; upon realising that Simon hadn't replied. Simon was not standing where Alan thought he would be.

Alan sighed and shook his head. Simon must have gone for a cigarette again. He said he had quit.

Alan looked back to the cadaver, once again, starting at the heart slowly checking each organ methodically and thoroughly.

'I swear that wasn't there when I checked before.' Alan said to himself, noticing scarring to the lungs.

He looked at the liver. It too was scarred and a little worse for wear, as if the young girl had been drinking for a good few years.

'How the hell did I miss that?' Alan said, confused by the sudden change. Taking a step back, Alan noticed, the entire body shape under the drape was different.

He reached over and took a corner of the material and lifted it up.

Alan shrieked as he unveiled Simon's face, the older

man's glassy eyes staring at the ceiling.

A Time of Our Own

The screaming alarm interrupted Matt's vivid dream about walking broccoli, much to his annoyance. His hand reached out from under the duvet and slapped the thing several times until it stopped making noise. He lay there for a moment before sitting up and yawning, looking towards where Toni was sleeping. She was lying face down, her hair snaking across the pillow in every direction, like some crazy medusa. He poked her a couple of times and she snorted and groaned, before waving him off. Matt got up and took a shower, before heading to his wardrobe and getting dressed in simple trousers and a long sleeve t-shirt, both of which were black. Toni was getting out of bed as he dressed; patting Matt on the head as she wordlessly walked past him and entered the bathroom.

Matt looked at the two duffle bags that they had packed the evening before and debated in his mind for a moment or so. Eventually, he crouched down and unzipped them both, looking through and checking the contents, making sure that everything they needed was inside.

'Hey, everything ok?' Toni asked as she walked out of the bathroom, rubbing her wet hair with a towel.

'Yeah, just wanted to check, didn't want to miss the appointment because we forgot something.' Matt said, zipping the bags back up.

After a few moments, Toni was also dressed, wearing

similar black trousers and a t-shirt. Her long brown hair was now in a French plait and she was jogging on the spot.

'Right,' Matt said, standing up. 'I think we are good to go.' Toni gave a firm nod and they both took one of the duffle bags each. They walked out of the door of their apartment and locked it securely behind them.

The morning was warm and sunny, so they decided to walk to their appointment as opposed to taking a taxi. It took them about half an hour, but their walk was at a fast pace, despite their luggage. They got to the Grenson Building with ten minutes to spare until their appointment, so they slowed down once they had entered the large glass doors.

Inside was the reception area, with both a young man and woman sitting behind the desk. The man was on the phone and looked deep in conversation, staring at his computer screen, so the woman looked up and smiled at them.

'Hello! Welcome to Grenson Industries,' She said, 'Do you have an appointment with us today?'

'Yes yes yes!' Toni said excitedly, turning to Matt. Matt fumbled about in his bag for a moment, before pulling out a couple of documents and passed them to the woman. She read them for a moment before typing some things into her computer. After a moment or two, she looked back at them and with a smile, gestured to the other side of the room.

'Please, this way.' She said. She walked over to a door on the far-left side of the reception, opening the door. Toni and Matt followed her and stepped through the doorway into the next room. The woman passed a small plastic card to Toni and smiled once again.

'Your membership says that you have been here multiple times before, so I am just going to assume you know what you are doing?'

'Yes, thank you.' Toni said with a smile and Matt gave an enthusiastic thumbs up.

'Well, please press the buzzer if you need anything and have a safe journey.' The woman said, before giving her own thumbs up to Matt and closing the door behind her.

Matt and Toni dropped their bags, unzipping them and taking the contents out and laying them on the floor. They spent a few moments in silence, slowly placing each separate piece onto themselves.

Both wore simple light gambesons, covered by a mail vest and leather plate armour. Their arms were covered by leather bracers and they strapped leather grieves to their legs. Toni put on two fingerless leather gloves, while Matt only put on one on his right hand. Matt then strapped a quiver full of arrows onto his back, before constructing his compound bow, which he held in his left hand.

Toni then helped him to strap his short-sword to his waist.

He then returned the favour and helped Toni to strap her one-handed sword to her belt. Toni carefully passed Matt a knife, which he slid into his boot. Toni strapped hers on her hip.

Finally, they securely placed their satchels on their

backs and took a few minutes to check each other, ensuring their straps were tight and secure.
Toni picked up the wrist band that was hooked into the terminal on the wall and fastened it around her wrist. She slotted the plastic card into the terminal and it scanned for a moment with a circular loading sign, which eventually turned into a smiling emoticon face.
'Greetings.' it said. 'Welcome to Grenson Industries. We hope that you have a pleasant journey. Have you used this facility before?'
Toni tapped 'Yes'.
'Would you like a reminder of the rules and features of our security systems?'
Toni tapped 'No'.
'Please select your time period and duration of trip.'
A keypad appeared on the screen with the numbers zero to nine, as well as zeroes in groups of two, three and four. Beneath those, were two more selections, one saying AD and the other BC.
'Still happy with what we decided Matt?' Toni asked.
'Yeah, I'm still good.' he replied.
'Alright then.' With that, Toni tapped in the numbers two-two and then AD. She then typed '5 hours' into the section under 'Duration'.
Another page opened and read:
'Would you like to continue from the last date you visited?' Toni tapped Yes.
The screen showed the spinning load bar for a moment before the smiley face appeared again. 'Please select your location.' This time a QWERTY keyboard appeared and Toni typed in England, North West.

'Please select your level of security before continuing. Due to cultures and events in this time period, a security rating of High is suggested.'
The face disappeared and several options popped up. The options read High, Medium High, Medium, Medium-low and low. Toni looked at Matt who nodded firmly. Toni turned back to the machine and tapped the Low option. A small warning popped up, repeating the same warning that the face had given earlier. Toni tapped the 'I understand and wish to continue' option and the popup closed.
'Thank you for making your choice. Please wait while the system loads.'
A small loading bar appeared on screen and began to count up from zero percent, increasing about two percent every second or so. Toni and Matt took a step back, stretching and shaking their limbs. They stood in the centre of the room, legs apart and arms by their side. As the bar got to ninety percent, they held hands and the room flooded with a brilliant white.

The first thing that Matt always noticed was how clean the air smelled. It was fresh, crisp and unsoiled. For Toni, it was the silence that surrounded them. No cars or planes, just the sound of rustling leaves and birds singing their hearts out. They stood, just as they had been in the room, now in a forest. The sun was streaming through the trees and the ground was damp from dew from early morning. They took a few moments, just breathing in the air and embracing the quiet.

'Right,' Matt said, 'which direction?' They looked around, considering the terrain and familiar landscape and worked out to head South. They walked slowly, constantly scanning their horizons, behind trees and listening to all the noises that surrounded them.
They came across a small stream which ran with clear water and they sat and drank, resting for a small while. Even the water had a fresher taste to it, so they drank their fill and filled a couple of canteens.
'When do you think we will get to the village?' Toni asked, looking around, admiring the trees and blue sky.
'At the pace we have been going, not long, I think.' Matt replied. 'We will get there before nightfall.'
They stayed at the stream for a few moments, before getting up and stretching, making their way down the large stones and onto a small dirt path.
They chatted quietly as they walked, mainly about the village they were walking to, including the storyteller they had befriended, Aethul. They wondered if Maedoc had given birth yet and if so, was it a boy or a girl.
Toni mentioned how she wanted to get another piece of venison that the village butcher sold, as she had taken a liking to it. It went well in a pie with leek and cabbage. The herbs and salts the butcher used to preserve the meat were unlike anything Toni had tried before, giving it an exquisite flavour.
Toni and Matt had become regular travellers through the village, visiting almost every time they came to this time period. The villagers had greeted them warmly and with kindness, even giving Toni and Matt odd jobs to do, like quests in a video game.

'Look,' Matt said, pointing at the large dead oak tree that hugged the corner of the path. 'Just around the corner.'

'Thank goodness,' Toni said. She put her hand to her face and pinched her nose. 'I hope that smell fades away soon though. It's making me gag.'

Matt sniffed the air and suddenly registered the smell. It was rancid, fetid. He hoped someone had just relieved themselves nearby after eating something that was probably not suitable for humans.

They crossed the small ford which passed over the path and walked along the line of trees, approaching the large boulder which hid the entrance to the village from the main path.

'God, why won't that smell just go away?' Toni said, half gagging. 'I was hoping to have smelled cooking food by now.' They walked around the boulder.

'Oh god, no...'

In front of them, no longer was the small village of friendly people, living in several mud and wattle huts with thatched roofs, with a large cooking pit in the centre. There were no villagers talking, eating and working, children playing hunting and sword fighting. No longer was there the smell of cooking venison and the sound of stories coming from Aethul and the promise of new life from Maedoc.

They entered the circle of the village, staring at the once standing buildings, now nothing but piles of burnt and charred wood. The ground was sodden mud, mixed with what Matt and Toni could only assume was blood.

Rotten food was scattered everywhere, the fire pit in the centre had been partially filled with stones. The village had been razed to the ground and there was no sign of anyone. Toni spent a few minutes attempting to rummage through some of the ash, finding very little, except a small ringlet, which she slotted onto her arm.
'Maybe…maybe they…' Toni stammered, panicking. 'Maybe they just left. Moved onto somewhere else.'
'Toni…' Matts' voice drifted over to her from just outside the village. 'We need to leave.'
Toni stood and looked around for him. He was walking back into the village from just beyond the wooden walls, from the path on the opposite side to where they had entered. He waved his hand towards where they had come from, not breaking his gaze to his front.
'We are leaving. Now.'

Toni looked in the direction in which he had just come, taking a few steps towards it.
'Toni,' she heard him snap. 'Don't.'
They stared at each other from across the village.
'Please,' Matt said.
Toni's heart raced. Her breathing became shallow and fast. With a deep breath, she turned and walked away from him, ignoring his voice and subsequent footsteps as he chased after her. She broke into a run, leaping over the fallen wall and through the gap it had left. She followed the footsteps that led away from the village, noticing there were more tracks than just Matts. There were many sets of footprints, as if a group of twenty or so had passed through this way.

The path Toni followed ran parallel to the village, turning after a few metres, leading to another path that descended down a small incline and entered a grouping of trees. Running the total length of the path, on either side were dozens of long sticks. On the end of these sticks were the severed heads.

Some of the heads were hanging from the sticks, held on by pieces of rope. The rope entered the mouth and passed through the hole in the neck, fastening them in place. Several of them swung gently in the slight breeze that also ruffled the hair of the impaled heads.

The heads were all slightly decomposed, though Toni was able to identify several of the villagers, including Maedoc. Not even the children of the village had been spared from being part of the vulgar display.

Toni ran to the side of the path and vomited. She spat several times, before retching again. She felt the presence of Matt stood behind her and took a few moments to compose herself.

Looking just a few feet back down the path, she could see another pile of vomit, from Matt when he had first encountered the sight.

'Just…down there…' Matt said, pointing slightly off to the side of the path, 'Are the bodies. They…have just been dumped in a shallow hole. There wasn't even anything covering them.'

'My God, why?' Toni asked the sky, 'I don't understand. This isn't right. Surely, it's not Romans?'

'I don't know. We need to leave this place. I have no fucking clue what the hell this is, but it's beyond us. This is more than we bargained for. We will have to report this event to the facility and they can block the area and event.'

They were both suddenly aware that a figure stood over by the small cluster of trees.

Toni stood straight and faced the figure who was a bit too far away to see clearly.

'Wait! Maybe that is a survivor! We can help them!' Toni said.

Matt pulled out a small pair of binoculars and passed them to Toni, who looked through them.

She could see very little of the figure's face and couldn't deem whether it was a man or woman.

Their hair was long and matted into thick clumps. They wore torn and tattered furs, possibly goatskin and on their head, they wore the skull and antlers of a stag.

The top of their face was obscured but their cheeks and chin were covered in a dark blue colouring.

The figures' hands were covered in what looked like black tar, which dropped off in thick long globules.

They stared directly at Matt and Toni, similar to how a cat stares at prey before they pounce.

The figure raised their arms and began to loudly chant in a language that the Grenson translator was unable to change to English. After a few moments of chanting, the figure let out a primal scream. Seconds later, there was a resonating scream from the trees and several figures ran out from the forest. These figures wore dirty and stained white clothes with hoods covering their heads. Most of the faces that Toni could see were also covered in blue colouring or beards.

These new figures waved swords and clubs above their heads as they howled and screamed like wild animals driven into a frenzy. One of them seemed to be brandishing a human head.

'Shit.' Matt said, 'Not Romans.'

He pulled an arrow out of the quiver and knocked it, drawing the bow.

He did this as more of a display of strength, not intending to let it loose. If he released the arrow then the Paradoxum would kick in and they would be redacted with a penalty.

'Toni, redact us. We need to get out of this situation and report it. We can come back before this. We can come back and see everyone alive again… We can warn them and they can leave before this all happens.'

Toni stared at the figures that had begun to move towards them, eventually snapping out of it and tapping the band on her wrist.

It beeped.

'Toni, Hurry up.'

'But...I…' She tapped it again, this time with more force. The device beeped again.

'It's not working.' She said, looking at Matt.

'What? What do you mean?'

Toni held her arm out in front of Matt and tapped the band again. Once more, it beeped.

'Brilliant. Trust our luck to get a faulty device. Ok, guess we have to do it this way.'

Matt raised the bow and let go of the arrow. It sailed through the air towards one of the figures who were slowly walking towards them. Matt and Toni watched the arrow, waiting for the moment it stopped inches from the human target and the blinding white dragged them back into the facility room.

***

The arrow hit the figure in the chest and they fell back onto the grass, ceasing movement.
Matt and Toni stood silent, their mouths hanging open.
'I just…killed them.' He stared at the body. 'Why didn't we redact?'
'Matt, somethings gone wrong. We need to get out of here. Find somewhere safe and try and work out what the hell is going on.' Toni said, drawing her sword and looking around the area.
The group of figures had started to run towards them but had to first clamber up a small incline to reach the path. Matt and Toni turned and ran back into the village, passing through briskly and keeping their eyes up. Matt could hear the sound of footsteps running through wet mud behind them, growing louder as the group descended upon them.
Matt and Toni ran a short distance down the path away from the village and Toni slapped Matt on the left shoulder. They made a sharp turn, disappearing into the woods in the hope of losing their pursuers.
The trees of the woodland were tall and thin, yet the brush was dense and lush. They made their way through the woods, moving low to the ground and stopping occasionally behind trees, peering back from where they came from, looking to see if they were still being pursued.

Toni ran and hid behind a tree, looking around for Matt, who was nowhere to be seen. They had lost each other in the panic of the chase, not ideal in their current situation, Toni thought.

The forest was still for a few moments, but Toni finally spotted movement a few metres away.

A single man, his face covered in dark blue colouring, his mud matted hair covered by a hood, slinked through the forest. He snarled as he moved and in his hand, he held a wooden club with a large stone at the end.

Breathing slowly and gently, Toni kept her hand on the tree and went down on one knee, gently sliding her sword back into the scabbard. She started to reach for her dagger, but a hand quickly moved around her mouth and she was pulled backwards, the man in front of her disappearing from her sight.

Toni was pulled downwards, into a deep ravine, the top hidden by large fern leaves and thicket. She pushed away from the hand that had grabbed her, took quick three steps forward and spun on her heel, drawing her sword and stood en-garde towards her assailant. Toni froze when she saw the hand belonged to a young girl who was visibly terrified.

The girl had a hood covering her head and a long cape that covered most of her body. Behind her, stood a tall, slender man dressed in mail armour, covered with an iron cuirass. He had an axe on his waist.

Further behind him, were three other figures. On the left, there was a young boy in simple peasant clothing with a satchel and to the right, a woman who was wearing a full suit of steel plate armour.

Sat on the floor between them, was a man who was wearing a long robe and, as much as Toni could not believe it, a tall pointed wizard hat. His robe was stained with blood, which ran from a huge gash across his chest. He was almost screaming in pain, biting down on a piece of wood as the woman shushed him and the young boy tried to stem the blood flow.
Toni finally noticed the last person in the gully was Matt, who was gesturing for Toni to put down the sword. He had a bloody lip.
'Please,' the young girl said, raising her hands. 'Please don't hurt us. We need help.'
Toni glanced at Matt who nodded assumingly and she sheathed her sword.
'What the hell is this?' Toni asked, looking towards the wizard.
Matt shrugged at Toni before he stepped over towards the wizard. The tall man stepped in front of him, his hand resting on the top of his axe. Matt sighed and stared at him.
'Let me see him dammit. She asked for our help,' Matt pointed at the young girl. 'I'm a nurse. I can help.'
After a moment of genuine contemplation, the man stood to the side and Matt quickly crouched next to the wizard and started to examine him.
'What happened? Be clear.' He asked, gently lifting the shredded robes, placing them back quickly when blood flowed out from the wound.
'We were ambushed by that...cult. Johnny was slashed by a guy with a sword.'
Johnny mumbled through the stick in pain, spitting it

out. 'Why didn't the security redact me?' he said, almost crying.

Matt looked at Toni, who stared back at him.

'We came across some people too, we tried to redact using the wrist band, but it didn't work.'

'Same with us,' the armoured woman said. 'We all tried but it didn't work.'

'I killed one of them,' Matt said, not looking up from the wound. 'But here we still are.'

'This doesn't make sense. The Paradoxum would pull us out if any of this happened. Why are we still here?' The young girl said.

'What security level did you choose?' Toni asked, not looking up from the wounded man.

'Medium High.' The young boy said.

'So, you should have been redacted the moment there was any sense of danger to any of you. The attacker wouldn't have even gotten close, let alone-' Toni pointed at the wounded man. '-that happen. Something has gone wrong at Grenson. An IT failure or maybe they have been hacked. Something is stopping us from leaving.'

'What do we do?' The young girl said, in a very quiet and scared voice.

There was a silence through the group, as everyone stared at the ground.

Matt spoke.

'I'm sorry. Johnny is dead.'

The entire group except Toni turned and gasped. Johnny lie, eyes closed, his head rested backwards and

a small dribble of blood ran out the side of his mouth.
'This wasn't supposed to happen!' The young boy said, his voice shrill. 'I want to go home! This was supposed to be a game! Like Dungeons and Dragons!'
Matt placed his hand on the boy's shoulder. He didn't know what to say.
All Toni and Matt could do was to remain silent as the group wept and held one another.
The group discussed what to do and it was agreed that, as the sun was starting to get low, it was best to wait until morning before they moved.
They stayed in the small gully, using the covering to stay hidden, covering Johnny's body with a cloak and several branches.
The other group huddled together to stay warm, while Matt and Toni did the same, but a few feet away.
Toni pointed at Matt's lip.
'What happened?'
'Oh, the woman in armour did that. It was my fault. I swung at her first when she grabbed me.'
Toni sniggered and rested her head back against his shoulder, closing her eyes only to find that sleep eluded her.
Toni lay awake all night, leaning against Matt as he slept against the side of the gully. His arm was around her shoulder and she pressed her cheek against it, taking in his warmth. He stirred slightly before going quiet. She sat, staring at the side of the gully until her eyes grew heavy and sleep finally took her.
They both woke early, just as the light of the morning began to filter through the canopy above them.

The Tall man was also awake and he quietly walked over.

'My name is Paul. The young girl is Lacy, the young lad is George and the woman who clobbered you-' he pointed at Matt, '- is Anya, my wife.'

'I'm Toni and this is Matt,' Toni replied quietly.

'Nice to meet you. Sorry it's not under better circumstances.'

Paul shrugged.

'Agreed.' He left it at that.

Matt looked at the others, their eyes opening and the memory of the previous night returned to them.

'You guys, seem to be like...a guild, I guess?' Matt asked. 'Like Dungeons and Dragons or an MMORPG?'

Paul nodded.

'Yeah, kinda. We do this once a week and just have small adventures, making up our own quests as we go along. Just a regular role play, but on location.'

Matt nodded.

'Makes sense as to why you had a wizard. No offence.'

'None taken,' Paul replied, 'Johnny was the most eccentric of us, but he didn't deserve what that cult did to him.'

'We don't necessarily know they are a cult.' Toni replied. 'Might just be an unknown sect of paganism.'

Paul shrugged, 'Ritual sacrifice sounds cultish to me.'

***

Once everyone was awake, they took their time digging a grave for Johnny. Using pieces of armour or their weapons, they managed to dig a hole about two feet deep. They placed the body inside and covered it over, using twigs and leaves to cover the soil.

The surrounding forest was full of bird song and rustling leaves, so Matt and Toni left the gully first, splitting up and scouting out the area. Once they deemed it all clear, they returned to the group and helped them out one by one.

'Where do we go?' Anya asked.

'Well, the village we usually visited has been destroyed,' Toni said, 'but I think there is another one a few miles east.' She looked at Matt for confirmation and he nodded.

'Alright then. Would you lead the way?' Anya asked, to which Toni turned and started the trek.

Walking slowly, taking their time to scan their horizons, through the trees and along the paths, Matt and Toni led the group for several miles. The sun beamed through the trees and a gentle wind cooled their skin.

Eventually, George spoke up.

'Can we stop and rest for a bit?' Toni looked around the area, making sure it was clear.

'Yeah, this is a good place to stop. If you need to relieve yourself, don't go too far.' She said as the others began to sit and stretch.

Toni walked a small distance from the group, making a small perimeter and keeping an eye out on the horizon. She came across George, who had broken away from the group and was sitting on a tree stump, drawing.

'Hey.' Toni said, as the boy looked up. He looked about sixteen she thought. She pulled out a cereal bar and broke it in half, passing some to George, who took with thanks and ate.

'Did you see the heads?' George asked quietly, not looking up at Toni.

'I did.'

'I'm an active gamer. I've played all the top titles, on all the best consoles. I've seen all the newest horror and action movies and TV shows.' He erased something with the end of his pencil.

'I especially liked the ones that had lots of blood and gore...' he trailed off.

'But seeing that...' he continued, 'seeing that was too much. I can't get it out of my head. I see it when I close my eyes. When I sleep. I'm starting to see them even when my eyes are open.'

Toni sat down.

'Somethings are not meant to be seen,' she said, putting her arm around the young boy. 'We will get out of here. They will fix the error and we will be redacted and you will return home. I promise.'

George looked up from his drawing and nodded.

'Thank you.'

There was a thud and Toni looked down at the spear that stuck out of George's chest. The young boy stared at the spear for a moment, before his head drooped forward.

'Shit!' Toni screamed, leaping to her feet and drawing her sword. A cultist leapt out of the bushes and ran screaming at Toni, blade held high.

In preparation for all their adventures, Matt and Toni had taken lessons and had watched countless hours of sword combat and archery videos. They even sparred together for countless weeks, honing their combat abilities until they were good in a fight. Both Toni and Matt were good fighters, but because of the security that came with the Paradoxum, they never dealt a killing blow until now. Until this point, the training had mainly been for exercise and fun.

This was the first time that Toni was going to fight for real and kill a living being.

Toni parried the man's first swing, knocking the rough blade to the side and returning with a swing. As Toni swung, she stepped past the man. There was a silence and then the sound of a body thudding to the ground. Toni had done it. She had won. She had killed.

She vomited.

Toni looked to George's body, removing the spear and laying him down flat on the ground. She ran her fingers over his eyes, shutting them and giving him a look of serenity. A shout of several voices suddenly broke through the air, from the direction of the group.

Toni jumped over the body of the man she had just killed and ran towards the noise.

Toni leapt over a fallen log and found the rest of the group struggling in battle.

Paul and Matt were both battling several of the cultists, both men shoving and swinging at their attackers. Matt fought with his short sword having discarded his bow. In the middle of the area, there were two dead cultists, one of which had been killed by Matt's arrow.

Anya and Lacy were against a tree, the armoured woman keeping herself in front of the young girl as a cultist attacked. Anya managed to get her sword thrust into her attacker's chest as they attacked and left themselves open.

Paul managed to swing his axe and catch one of the cultists in the shoulder, sending him falling. With a yell, Paul swung the axe again and the sound of the cracking skull pierced the air.

Toni leapt towards the last couple of the attackers and struck one on the back of the knees, sending him falling down. Toni thrust to the fallen body and ended it.

The other cultists, now outnumbered, ran from the group, disappearing into the forest.

Matt ran to Toni, stopping to pull the arrow out of the body in the centre.

'Hey, are you alright?' Matt asked quietly.

'I...uh.' She cleared her throat. 'I killed someone. Actually, two now. George is dead.'

The colour drained from Matt's face briefly, before he took a breath.

'It's ok, you're ok.' Matt kissed Toni on the forehead. 'You did what you had to. We all did.' He looked at the others who were talking between themselves.

'Where is he?'

Before Toni could answer, Paul walked over.

'Have you seen George?' He asked.

Toni opened her mouth to answer but her face gave it away.

Lacy broke down crying and both Paul and Anya swore loudly.

They returned to bury George, again only digging a shallow grave and covering it as best they could.

They continued their trek in near silence.

Lacy walked up next to Toni and tugged at her arm.

'Thank you for being there with George at the end. He was a good guy...' She said.

'I couldn't save him,' Toni replied. 'I killed the man who killed him, but that's nothing.'

'It's everything.' Lacy said, flashing Toni a smile. 'Thank you.'

'How far until the village?' Anya asked Matt.

'Not far, another mile or so.' He answered. 'We should get there long before nightfall and then hopefully someone will be able to help us.'

'Good.' Anya looked at Matt's bow. 'By the way, you are a good shot. I'm glad we came across you two. I don't think we would have done so well on our own.'

'Thanks, we both have a passion for this type of adventure, though…without the killing.' Matt replied with a grimace.

There was the sound of snapping twigs and arrows flew between the two, hitting several trees instead of them.

'Dammit, Not again!' Paul shouted.

'Run!' Toni yelled. Everybody broke into a sprint.

They all heard the sound of bellowing and screaming from behind them, as a dozen cultists emerged from their hiding places.

Anya's foot caught on something and she fell, landing hard on her front. By the time she had pulled herself up, the cultists were on her. She quickly pulled out a knife and threw herself at one of them, thrusting the blade

into their neck. She attempted the same move on a different cultist, but they quickly side-stepped her attack and decapitated her with a single swing.
Paul screamed and charged them, his axe held high. The others watched as he disappeared behind several of the cultists and the sound of him fighting slowly grew quieter.
'We need to run. Fast.' Matt said.
Toni pulled at Lacy's arm.
'Come on Lacy. You have to run.'
The young girl didn't move. She was frozen to the spot, staring towards the large group of cultists, who gleefully danced around the body of her friend.
'Lacy, please, we have to go.' Matt pleaded.
Lacy began to sob and fell to her knees.
'Please, get up!' Toni shrieked. She attempted to get the girl back onto her feet, but every time she tried, the girl's body went limp and fell back to the ground.
'Matt, help me!'
They tried to carry Lacy together, but found it was impeding their speed and after a few metres, she slipped from their grasp. Matt looked back down the path and then at Toni, who was still desperately trying to get the girl up. The cultists had started moving toward them.
'Toni, we need to go...we have to leave her. We can't carry her. They will catch us.'
Toni glared at Matt with so much anger; it sent a shiver down his spine. He gently stepped forward and put his hand on her shoulder. The cultists were nearly upon them.
'Toni. We have to go.'

Toni stared at the cultists and then tried to get Lacy up again. No success once more. The cultists were yards away. Toni stared at Lacy's sad glassy eyes, as she sobbed to the air.

'Fuck!' Toni screamed, before turning and running.

Matt gently touched the top of Lacy's head.

'I'm sorry.' He whispered before he too turned and ran.

Matt and Toni got a small distance away, before stopping and looking back. They could still see Lacy, now surrounded by the dancing and bellowing cultists. They watched as the cultist leader, the person with deer antlers on their head, walked towards the group. The circling group stopped and watched as the leader passed through their ranks and approached the young girl in the centre.

The leader stepped up behind the sobbing girl and grabbed her by the hair, pulling her head back in a sharp yank. Lacy sobbed as a blade was placed against her throat and she let out a final loud sob as the blade was slowly dragged across her soft skin.

Blood flowed free from the cut, soaking the ground moments before Lacy's body followed it.

Toni and Matt turned, running away as tears streamed down their faces.

They ran to the village, not stopping until they passed through the outer gate and into what they hoped would be their salvation.

The scent of decay and fire greeted them.

'Well, that's just brilliant.' Matt said as he kicked a

bucket with so much force it splintered.
'What do we do now?'
He looked at Toni, who was facing away from him. She remained silent. Matt swallowed hard and stepped over to her.
'I'm sorry. I'm sorry I made you leave Lacy.'
Toni turned and, using the momentum of her turn, slapped Matt hard across the face. Her eyes seethed with hatred.
Matt carefully put his hand against his stinging cheek and gently nodded, stepping back. Before he could get too far, Toni pulled him into a hug and they both began to cry.

Toni looked around at the mess of burnt houses and corpses. Several of the corpses were missing heads, just like the ones in Aethul and Maedoc's village.
She looked at the band on her wrist and pressed it again. It beeped but still nothing happened. She sighed, looking at Matt who was pacing back and forth.
'Matt. I'm sick of running.' She said, quietly.
'What do you mean?' He asked, rubbing his temple, chasing away a headache.
'I mean, we fight back. We find this cult and we kill them. One by one if we have to. Kill them, run, or attack all out and die. I don't care. I want to go and kill those bastards and stop them from doing this again.'
She gestured at the burnt village.
Matt stood, his hands on his hips, looking around at the destruction.
After a few moments, he nodded.

As darkness grew, they heard chanting and drumming coming from within the forest. The pure dark sky, though full of stars and the moon, was gently lit by the orange glow of a large fire from within the trees. They both agreed that is where they should head to find the cult.

They rested for a short while, building a small fire to warm themselves, before eating some cereal bars and finally, they checked their weapons and armour.

Toni spent a few moments, psyching herself up, forcing herself to remember the faces of Lacy, Anya, Paul, George and even Johnny.

'Matt. I'm ready.' Toni said. Matt stood and turned to her.

'Let's do it,' he said. 'Let's avenge our friends.'

They spent a few moments, mixing water and mud together, before smearing it over their faces and their armour, dulling the leather shine. Matt kicked out the fire and the darkness of the night engulfed them.

They moved silently through the forest, following the sound of the drums and chanting, soon being able to see the glow of the large fire that sat in the centre of a makeshift camp.

They stopped on the edge of the clearing, using the trees and bushes for cover, watching the shadowy figures dancing like beasts around the fire.

The stag head person stood between the fire and the dancers, screaming and chanting at the flames. Toni tapped Matt on the shoulder and pointed.

There was a guard standing away from the fire, just

beyond the edge of the camp, facing out into the darkness.

He stood right on the edge of the light from the fire, on the precipice of the darkness.

Moving through the dark, Toni and Matt slowly moved until they were crouched almost directly in front of the guard, hidden behind a small shrub. They waited a few moments, holding their breath at times and eventually, the guard turned and began to watch the ritual.

'Go.' Matt whispered. Toni stepped out from behind the shrub and crept towards the guard.

Creeping up behind him, Toni held her breath and ignored the putrid body odour, before slowly standing straight.

She grabbed the man in a single movement, covering his mouth and drawing her dagger across his throat. The man twitched in her arms for a few moments, before going limp. Toni carefully placed the body down and wiped the blood on her dagger onto the man's clothing. She looked up, to see another cultist standing over her, brandishing a sword. They raised it to strike but fell after an arrow thudded into their skull.

Toni caught the body as it fell and gently placed it next to the other. Toni breathed out heavily, looking towards the darkness of the forest. A moment later, a hand tapped her shoulder.

'Hey, got you covered.' Matt said as he moved into position next to her.

'Thank you.' she whispered.

The drumming grew louder and louder, as did the chanting. They watched from the shadows as a man was brought out, bound and gagged and placed in front of the fire.

'God, that's Paul,' Matt said. 'What do we do?'

Toni stared at the now bloody and cut up man, her mind racing.

'Go, go now. We can attack before...'

Before Toni was able to finish her sentence, Paul's bonds were cut and he was grabbed by both arms by two large men. Ignoring his screams, the men pulled on Paul's arms until they popped and came out of the sockets. The person with the antlers walked in front of the screaming Paul and raised a club above their head, holding it there for what seemed like an impossibly long time. They brought it down on top of Paul's head, which caved and sprayed blood onto the floor.

The cultist leader pulled a serrated knife out from their robes and plunged it into Paul's chest, sawing for a few moments, eventually tearing out his heart.

Paul's body was then lifted high by the large men and tossed onto the fire, sending thousands of embers dancing into the night sky.

The cultist leader took the heart and waved it in the air, spraying around globules of clotting blood. They held the heart with both hands, before sinking their teeth into it, ripping a chunk out and swallowing it.

'Fuck.' Matt whispered.

'We could have saved him if we were faster.' Toni said, turning to face Matt, who nodded gently.

They sat in the shadows for a moment, in quiet shame, before Matt shifted slightly.

'Let's do this,' He said, 'wait for my signal.'

They shared a passionate kiss, before parting and heading to opposite sides of the camp.

Matt reached the back of a large tent, making his way along the side of it, sticking to the shadows.

Carefully, he climbed up onto the top of an overturned cart next to the tent, pulling an arrow out from the quiver.

Knocking it and drawing the bow, he breathed deeply and loosed it, aiming for one of the larger men in the centre.

It hit them in the chest and they fell with a yell, crashing into another of the cultists and they both landed on the fire, screaming as the flames engulfed them.

Immediately he drew another arrow and loosed it towards the person with the stag head, who was grabbed by another cultist and shoved out of the way.

The arrow found its mark in the throat of the cultist and the stag headed person screamed something in their unknown language.

The confusion of the initial attack ceased as the group all turned their attention to Matt, who now stood and drew yet another arrow.

This was the signal.

Toni leapt into action, running up to the cultists who now faced away from her, striking several of them on the back of the knees with her sword. They fell onto their backs, one having both legs severed from the force of Toni's strike. Using her dagger, she quickly finished them off, just as the other cult members reacted.

After being attacked on both sides, the cultists yelled

and separated both ways. Matt chose the nearest cultist and loosed an arrow towards them. The cultist ducked the arrow, though it hit the woman running behind him. Matt jumped off the cart and moved backwards, disappearing into the night.

Toni engaged the closest attacker, slashing at their torso and using the momentum of her movement to carry to the second cultist, striking in the neck with her dagger. She parried an attack by a third cultist, pushing them back into the others, causing them to stumble over. Toni took this chance to quickly run backwards, also disappearing into the night.

The cultists bellowed and shouted in confusion, spreading out to try and find Toni and Matt. Suddenly, an arrow felled one of them, striking from the darkness where Toni had vanished into. Matt ran forward, losing another and hitting a second cultist.

A couple of the cultists at the rear turned, expecting the same tactic and for Toni to attack from the other side once again.

Instead, Toni raced past Matt, striking as he loosed a third arrow. She cut down two of the cultists before they even turned around, striking at the others who heard her coming. Matt took down the last couple that faced him, one with an arrow and the other with his short sword.

It was over in a matter of moments.

Toni saw movement from behind her and dodged out of the way as the cultist leader thrust a knife at her. Toni slashed the leader's leg and they fell, landing hard on the ground next to the fire.

The cultist leader groaned and held their leg, blood pouring from the wound. Toni and Matt stood over them, both panting heavily.

Toni grabbed the deer antlers and tore the headdress off the leader. Beneath was an elderly woman, possibly in her late sixties to seventies. The woman looked up at them, no fear in her eyes, only what seemed like an intense hatred.

Matt nodded at Toni, who raised her sword.

The leader spat and said something in their language, seconds before Toni swung.

***

Toni awoke to the familiar sound of birds chirping and a warm beam of the sun shining through the crack in the door. She slowly sat up and looked around the small cottage. She could hear Matt working outside, sawing away at some wood. She got up, taking time to wash her face, tie up her grey hair and change into her work clothes, which included a worn leather apron, full of small tools.

She stepped outside into the fresh spring air and saw Matt hard at work, his long hair tied up and his beard full of sawdust.

'Please be careful, you aren't a young man anymore. Have you been awake long?' Toni asked.

'A small while,' he said with a chuckle, 'Just wanted to make an early start. Hope I didn't wake you.' Toni shook her head.

She went and collected a couple of eggs from the coop and checked on their leeks and cabbages. Farmer Fial walked past their house and waved, to which Toni waved back.

'You going to the village later?' Fial called out.

'Maybe. If we can hobble along!' Toni shouted back.

Fial laughed and walked away, waving as he did so. Matt walked over and passed her a cup of hot water flavoured with rosemary and lavender.

They stood for a moment enjoying the gentle breeze and the gentle rustling of leaves.

'All things considered,' Matt said, 'this has been nice.'

Toni took her husband's hand and squeezed it gently, remembering those lost, but also the peaceful and idyllic life that had followed.

'It really has.' she said, as the sun warmed her skin and the birds sang loudly.

Slap

Becca tapped her husband on the shoulder as he stared at himself in the mirror.
'Hey Luke, you alright?'
With a small grunt, he moved his face closer to the mirror and pulled down on his bottom eyelid, examining his eyeball.
'Yeah, I'm alright. Probably just drank too much.' Luke said with a sigh, before sticking out his tongue and grimacing.
Becca placed the back of her hand to his forehead, pulling it away again quickly.
'God, you are burning up. You might have the flu.'
'I'll be fine.' Luke said, as he ran the cold tap and splashed the water over his face.
Becca stared at him for a moment, knowing how stubborn he was in regards to his own health. She turned back to the sink and began to brush her teeth, secretly hoping her husband was going to take something before bed.
Luke was already in bed and seemingly asleep by the time she had finished taking off her makeup and undressed into her cotton pajamas.
These ones, featuring a small teddy bear, were her favourites. Becca climbed into bed, kissing Luke gently on the top of the head, before settling back and picking

up her book, which she read for ten minutes, before setting it down and switching off the light.

Sunlight filtered through the gap in the curtains as Luke bolted awake, gasping for air, before rolling over to the edge of the bed and vomiting right onto the new carpet. He rolled back; taking several deep breaths and tore the bedsheets off of his sweat-drenched body. It took him three attempts to sit up, but even then, the room spun like crazy.
Once he had managed to get into a sitting up position, Luke carefully swung his legs over the side of the bed, placing his feet on either side of the pool of vomit. Heaving himself up using the table next to the bed, he slowly staggered to the bathroom, where he vomited again, but this time in the toilet. He splashed himself with cold water and brushed his teeth, feeling slightly better at this time.
'Probably just something I ate.' He thought to himself.
 It was at this moment, he looked back at the bed, realising that Becca was not there. Luke looked at his watch, seeing that it was about nine-thirty and was also Sunday. She was probably downstairs dealing with the little monsters that they called children. He took a shower, deciding not to shave, before dressing in a simple combination of a grey shirt and dark blue jeans. Luke sighed, looking at the vomit by the bed, hoping he would be able to get it cleared up before Becca noticed. He just had to get a sponge and bucket from the kitchen

first. Passing by the bedrooms of his children, he stuck his head in. Both of their beds were empty as well, so maybe they would be distracting Becca.

Luke quickly descended the stairs and walked through the hall towards the kitchen. Just before he entered the kitchen, his mind quickly pondered on how quiet it was, especially if the kids were up.

'Hey, hon?' he called out in an attempt to gauge where she was. He received no reply and upon entering the kitchen, he found it to be empty. He made a 'Hmm' sound, before walking around the kitchen island, fixing his eyes on the cupboard with the mop in.

Luke yelled loudly as his foot went into something wet and warm. He almost swore loudly as he hopped back, grabbing at his wet foot. He looked down, before grabbing a towel and using it to clean the cold liquid off his foot. Just behind the island, out of view from the door, was a large gelatinous mass of red and brown liquid, about the size of an exercise ball.

'What the hell is that?' Luke exclaimed, to himself mainly. He stared at the mess on the floor, wondering what the hell it was. It wasn't vomit, nor was it any kind of food or sewage. Maybe it was something that the kids had created from a 'magical' concoction of things. 'Becca?' Luke called out, this time a lot louder, hoping she would have answers.

'Natalie? Benny?' There was no answer to his shouting. Maybe they had gone to the park? Surely there would be a note on the fridge though?

He moved from the kitchen into the living room, to find it empty, yet the television was on, displaying static. In front of the television were two more gelatinous blobs, side by side. The blob on the left had Bunny the Bear next to it.

He stared at both of the blobs for a few moments, suddenly seeing that they were ever so slightly pulsing. 'What the hell?' He said, the words catching in his throat.

Luke ran back into the kitchen, to look at the first blob again. He saw the evidence of breakfast, a few sliced fruits and some toast that had popped out of the toaster. This blob pulsed too, seemingly to slowly move towards him.

With a shriek, Luke bolted out of the kitchen and scrambled up the stairs, racing to his mobile, dialling nine-nine-nine.

The line rang for a few moments, as Luke fidgeted in the empty room.

The ringing stopped and the line was suddenly disconnected. He tried again, only to be disconnected instantly. Luke swore loudly, before running down the stairs again and flinging open the front door, getting outside for a better signal. After a moment of holding his phone to the sky, he tried the emergency services again, only to be cut off once more.

Phone in hand still, he sprinted towards number thirty, where family friend Kieran lived. Luke ran up the path at such a pace, he slammed right into the door before

banging on it with his fists.
After a minute or two, though it felt more like twenty, the door opened and Kieran stood there. His face carried an expression of confusion, while he still wore a dressing gown and held a cup of coffee.
'Luke, what the hell?' he said, his voice full of sleepiness.
'I need you. At the house. It's Becca and the kids. Please.' Luke said, barely taking a breath.
Without a pause, Kieran dropped his mug and ran to his cupboard, throwing his dressing gown to the floor. He pulled out a bag and quickly put on his paramedic jacket. He was out the door in seconds and ran with Luke back to the house.
'Luke, what happened? Give me as much detail as you can.' Kieran said.
Luke entered the house first and directed Kieran to the kitchen, his hands up in the air.
'I don't know...look, just…look.' Luke said, not sure exactly what to say to Kieran as he stared at the blob on the kitchen floor.
There was the sound of a wet slap and a thud.
Luke looked up, towards the door of the kitchen, to see the medical bag on the floor and yet another blob.

The Drifting Wars

'Yuck, I hate that smell.'
I watched as the door in front of Jenkins slid open, the odour that at first was only slight, suddenly washed over us, causing several of the squad to gag. I swallowed hard and took the first step through the door, passing from one ship to another. The gargantuan Titan Class Transporter seemed to groan under its own mass, despite being in the weightlessness of space. The smell was now really quite overpowering, a mix of Sulphur and what I assumed was some form of faeces, most likely human.

The lights in the ship buzzed and flickered, doing a dance like the hokey-cokey. On, off, on and off, throwing shadows violently through the room. I clicked on my torch and looked around, checking the shadows and small corners. The rest of my squad followed my example, chasing away the darkness wherever they could with their torches. Jenkins sighed heavily, swallowed and raised his gun to his shoulder, watching the now lit corners and ceiling as we moved through the ship.

'It's ok, you're not really here. You are on a hot beach at the resort islands,' He quietly said to himself, more than once.

Sal laughed and bumped him with her elbow.

'C'mon dude, try and have a bit of backbone. Ain't

nuffin going to get ya.'
I listened intently for several moments, trying to get through the noise of the ship's buzzing engines and groaning hulking metal. There were no other sounds I could pick up. Nothing out of the ordinary. I waved my hand forward and we headed deeper into the ship, keeping our eyes on the walls, ceilings and ventilation. We were venturing into the carrier because our ship, the Clorha, had picked up a distress signal four hours ago. The Titan Cruiser had been spinning through space for several days, according to the timestamp of the signal. We relayed the signal back to Command and in response, we were ordered to investigate and, if necessary, mount a rescue mission.

As we passed through the darkened hallways, following the arrowed signs to the food hall, the odour grew stronger with each hesitant step. Upon finding the door that entered into the food hall, we stopped and grouped up. Sal pressed the button on the left side. The door slid open and I stepped through. The floor instantly became tacky and soft and my feet required extra effort to move them. This was a common occurrence on a ship like this and now walking would be a lot more difficult. I prayed we wouldn't have to run.
'There it is!' exclaimed Peter, his shrill voice breaking the silence, causing myself and several others of the group to flinch.
The youth started to run towards the circuit breaker on

the far wall, seconds before the floor taffy slowed him to a painful crawl. He reached the box eventually and started pulling out his toolbox and getting to work, muttering to himself as he did so. The time between him reaching the box and starting his work was uncomfortable, as the darkness played games with our minds.

There was a sudden and very loud hum, before the lights burst into life, momentarily blinding us as we threw our hands in front of our eyes to protect them. I gently opened my eyes, blinking often to adapt to the light.

'Oh god!' I heard Nancy exclaim.

I looked to the floor, knowing what to expect from a floor this sticky.

Bodies were strewn around, most of them grotesquely eviscerated. Many sat at the tables, dinner plates in front of them, utensils in their hands.

'They must have been eating at the time.' Someone said. I wasn't paying enough attention to know who. Other bodies were closer to the walls and exits, most likely as they had attempted to run. There were even some underneath the tables, where it seems like the victims had gone to hide.

Unfortunately, the crew of the ship had consisted of entire families, so there were also children among the dead.

I forced myself to look and check ID's, giving permission to my squad to pass if they were not comfortable doing so.

The walls and ceiling of the hall were covered in the thick, brown webbing that we had become so used to seeing. Oily liquid dripped off of it, the source of the foul odour emanating itself through the ship.

'Right…' I said, clearing my throat. 'We need to find the source of the distress signal.'

'Sir…' Peter spoke up, 'I think I have found it. It's…there.' With that, the boy pointed.

'What?'

I followed his finger and my eyes finally met the small flashing beacon, partially hidden underneath the corpse of what I think was a woman.

'Captain…' Jenkins said, his voice hoarse, 'These bodies, most have Arthro wounds but…they look slightly decomposed…as if it's been a few weeks. We only picked up the distress signal four hours ago… and it had only been active for a week or so.'

'I need you to be clear, Jenkins. I need to know that you are thinking what I am.' The Medic opened his mouth, but he could only manage a sharp nod.

'Shit,' I said, pulling my gun over my shoulder, 'Together, now!' Everyone ran over as best they could through the sticky floor.

The ten of us stood in a tight circle; our guns aimed outwards, eyes and torches on the walls and ceiling. How had I been so idiotic? This was a blatant trap and we walked right into it.

The low hum of the engines was suddenly

overwhelmed by the familiar screeching of the Arthro, followed by the sound of scurrying reverberating throughout the ventilation.

There was sudden movement behind us as an Arthro dropped from the ceiling and into the middle of the circle. Before any of us could turn in reaction, the Arthro scurried and wrapped around Jenkins, its mandibles clamping around his helmet, while its legs tore into the armour that contained the rest of his body. I raised my gun and fired at the creature, but not before there was a sickening crunch as the Arthro chewed its way through Jenkins' helmet and skull, his scream cut out by a surge of thick dark blood. Everyone else turned and opened fire, the creature screeching as it died, still entwined around my former soldiers' body, which then fell to the wet floor.

There were more loud screeches and Arthro began to pour out of the ventilation shafts around the room.

'Open fire. Get to the door! We need to get back to the Clorha!' I barked. In the partial circle, we sustained continuous fire and slowly moved towards the door, keeping the screeching creatures at bay. They charged and clawed at us multiple times, trying to break the circle, but most either died or retreated back due to the barrage of bullets. We killed dozens before reaching the door, but even more swarmed through the ventilation, almost as if they were fighting between themselves to get to us first.

I pulled out a combustion grenade and threw it into the

furthest corner of the room. It landed and disappeared behind several of the Arthro. After a moment, the grenade burst and flames engulfed the creatures. The flames quickly spread, engulfing the room, setting the bodies and Arthro alight. They screeched and bellowed as they burnt, the heat blistering and popping their fleshy skin.

Limited issue Combustion grenades are designed to start an unstoppable fire that will only go out when it has burnt every available fuel source or is doused with a specific coolant. They had been banned by the Governmental Collection (GC) for around fifty or so years for obvious reasons, but have since the war began, been permitted for use by select teams, mine included.

By the time my squad had reached the door of the food hall, there were only six of us left. Those who had fallen had fallen prey to the Arthro, having been caught by their legs and torn apart or devoured. The youngest woman in the group, Helen, had been dragged away screaming by one of them, despite all our best efforts. We lost sight of her in an instant, but her screaming echoed through the cruiser until we reached the airlock to our ship. We had to leave all the bodies to the fire, even those from my squad, but we had their numbers on file, so a record of them was kept, though that wasn't any comfort to their families.

I waited as each of my squad entered the airlock, until I

was the only one left. First in, last out. That was my personal rule. As I was about to board the ship, I stopped and turned back towards the cruiser innards. I watched as Arthro poured down the hallway, along the floor, walls and ceiling. Behind them, almost as if it was playing a game of tag, followed the raging fire.
I fired several rounds, killing a couple of the creatures as they managed to outrun the fire and get too close for comfort. Their bodies were engulfed by the hungry flame as they stopped dead. I stepped back and the door of the Clorha slid shut just as the fire licked against the door. There was a hum and a jolt as the ship jerked and broke away from the titan. I stood at the door, watching through the window as the ship's internal structure began to collapse in on itself, destroying the nest within. I guess that could constitute a victory for the GC against the Arthro.

***

I sat at my desk, fiddling with the silver half-heart locket that I wore around my neck.
'Hey codger, who owns the other half?' A voice asked. It was the pilot of the Clorha, Naomi.
'Hm?' I snapped back into the room and turned my chair to face her.
'Sorry, just thinking. My daughter Katie has the other half.'
She nodded, looking down, rubbing her neck.
'Makes sense I should have realized. Sorry.'

'It's alright.' I placed the locket back around my neck. 'My half has her name on it, her half has my name. I gave it to her on her tenth birthday. She loved it and never took it off.'

'Sounds like you were a good dad.'

'I tried to be...I don't know if I was or not. I feel like I missed too much. Too many years floating through space, fighting a war away from home.'

'She treasured a gift you gave her. She loved you. That's all you need to know to answer that, you twit.' Naomi said, patting the photo I had of my family on my desk.

My wife and daughter had been travelling from Earth to the base planet Zarion when their ship had disappeared. All traces of it had been lost during its journey and, despite dozens of searches, nothing of it was ever found. Since the war had started, this was a common occurrence, especially for ships that were not travelling with an escort warship or fighters.

Ships would get attacked and swarmed by the Arthro, which usually resulted in the ship detonating or being scuttled.

My daughter and wife were dead; I had no other choice but to accept that and so I chose to kill as many of those damn monsters as possible.

'What happened on that cruiser? I haven't seen you this rattled since I ate your yoghurt.'

I ran my hand through my hair and groaned. 'I have no freaking idea. Those damn monsters set up a bloody trap...somehow. I didn't think they were intelligent enough to do that.'

'They aren't. They are stupid animals...like pigeons.' Naomi said, walking around my desk to my side, peering at my screen.

'That signal was turned on seven days ago and we picked it up eight hours ago. All of the bodies we witnessed had been dead for weeks. They activated it. They knew it would bring someone. They laid in wait and then attacked. They planned it.' All I could do was sit there with my arms folded.

'I mean, it may have been a survivor who activated it, before the Arthro got to them.' She said, with a shrug.

'Kid, you know that those beasts don't leave any survivors at all. They hunt them down and tear them to shreds.'

'Yeah…' Naomi said, sticking her tongue out in a grimace. It was an agreement from experience.

Our ship beeped, turning Naomi's attention back to her duties.

'Sorry Michael. Got to get back to the bridge. I left Norman up there and he'll probably pilot us into the sun.'

I turned and waved as she left my office.

I turned my chair again but stopped short, my mechanical leg freezing in place. I sighed, giving it a whack with my fist. It whirred for a second and then a moment later, moved as if natural. I finally completed my turn, looking back to my computer and brought up the file I had on the Arthro. I read almost every document that we had on them and nowhere, not once, did it ever mention that they had ever set a trap or shown any sense of strategy in order of battle, aside from random, swarming attacks.

I clicked another file and pulled up the known anatomy of the Arthro.

The easiest way to describe them is to compare them to a centipede, hence the name Arthro, short for Arthropod.

They have dozens of legs, depending on their size, which is usually about that of a Labrador. Their length can vary, but they are usually about five to six-foot-long. At their head, they have large antennae and large vice-like mandibles with no visible eyes. Despite the supposed lack of eyes, they are able to spot prey from far away and follow it for a long distance.

The final, creepier feature of the Arthro was their skin. Unlike other insects and myriapods, their skin is like human flesh that is pale and sickly beige, due to their dark brown blood.

They are damn fast and strong, but can be taken down by several good shots; especially if you hit them in the head. They swarm like ants in battle, showing little care for their own wellbeing and seem constantly ravenous, able to tear apart and devour a human within mere seconds.

The war against the Arthro had started eight years ago,

in the year 4514 AD. It had begun when a cruise ship, which had been on a pleasure trip to the Outer Resort planets, was attacked.

The ship had been hit by an unidentified object, which was eventually revealed to be a large cocoon-like structure, about the size of a bus. Once it had collided with the ship and breached the hull, humans made first contact with the Arthro, as they swarmed out of the cocoon and massacred the thirteen thousand people on board. One of the crew members managed to send a distress signal and within a few hours, the GC first response unit had dropped onto the ship in an attempt to rescue survivors and clear out the creatures. This unit consisted of fifty of the greatest elite soldiers the GC had to offer, known as the Colossi Invictus. Outfitted with the best armour, weaponry and tactics, the unit had served a number of years and had participated in several skirmishes, wars and uprisings, entering the front lines and leaving without losing a single member or suffering any injuries.

To many on Earth, they were considered Gods of Warfare.

They were the first official combat unit to engage the Arthro. They lasted fifteen minutes.

As a result of their loss, the ship was destroyed by the six thousand foot long Leviathan Class Warship, Gorganite, which boasted twenty dreadnought cannons, as well as two hundred thousand crew members.

After the GC had scanned a nearby planet, believing it

was the source of the attack, an Arthro nest was discovered on it. The planet was then also destroyed by Gorganite, the dreadnaught cannons splitting the core with hundreds of titanium point shells. After that, several more planets were discovered with Arthro nests within them and the number of cocoon attacks on ships began to increase.

After the Gorganite was struck by several cocoons, a three-day long battle resulted in victory for humanity and the GC, at a loss of seven thousand soldiers and an estimated forty thousand Arthro. After this, the GC officially declared war on this seemingly unlimited enemy and the first Arthro-Human war began.

After this first battle, the war ramped up in intensity fairly quickly. The number of Arthro seemed to almost quadruple in a week and the number of attacks on ships, as well as battles on planet surfaces, started to become a daily occurrence. The death toll for the GC quickly reached over a million within a month. Since then, the death toll had been steeply climbing.

The intensity of this led the way for several different tactics and plans being implemented throughout the years, none of which resulted in any form of victory for either side.

After a year of war, the civilian planet of Polea was invaded by a single mountain-sized cocoon, home to several billion Arthro. The defences of the capital city Senea were overrun within minutes, as were the military forces that set up several blockades. The Arthro then swarmed the planet, killing billions of civilians. After this loss, the GC's priority went from pushing the Arthro back into space, to wiping them out in full genocide. To do this, the GC quadrupled their efforts to find and burn the homeworld of the Arthro. Millions of soldiers were recruited across the Collection, thousands of ships were built and hundreds of planets had been destroyed as the GC had searched for the Arthro homeworld.

So far, there have been a few planets that scientists have argued to have been the origin planet, but the Arthro keep coming, so most feel like it is still out there somewhere, waiting to be found in the inky darkness of space.

I had been in the GC army for about five years now, working my way up to the rank of Captain. My first contact with the Arthro was the land assault on Jernal-5. I was in the first wave, of about five thousand soldiers who were dropped on the planet's surface. The GC wanted to avoid destroying the planet, due to the vast resources it contained, deeming it essential for the war effort.

The initial plan was for the first wave to land and create a boundary of defence, so artillery and armoured vehicles could then be lowered in without being overwhelmed. From there, the planet would be swept sector by sector and all Arthro would be systematically wiped out.

The operation started off well, with the infantry creating a strong defence, firing in volleys and erecting several automatic gun emplacements. The resistance from the Arthro was light at first, with only a few dozen being present on the initial drop.

It was about thirty minutes into the operation when everything went to hell.

The armour was minutes away from being lowered onto the planet's surface when the ground had begun to shake in a 7.2 Richter earthquake. In a matter of moments, the surface of the planet had cracked open and thousands upon thousands of Arthro flooded out of the planet's crust and immediately overwhelmed the defences. The automatic guns, capable of firing ten thousand rounds a minute, mowed down hundreds of the creatures but were quickly swarmed and destroyed by the sheer number of Arthro.

The Arthro seemed to have no care for their own wellbeing, throwing themselves at the hail of bullets and clambering over the corpses of their kin. Because of this lack of self-preservation that they displayed, the GC suffered extremely heavy casualties quicker than anyone could have predicted. Command was forced to abandon the mission and implement an emergency evacuation. Out of the five thousand soldiers dropped, only nine hundred were extracted. The rest were torn apart during the chaotic battle that preceded the evacuation. After the failure of the operation, the GC was forced to obliterate the planet, instead of leaving it to the enemy.

I was severely wounded, losing my right leg and was slashed across the face by one the Arthro, which left me with a large scar, as well as only twenty-five percent vision in my left eye. I only survived because a medic from the evac ship gave up her space for me, choosing to remain on the planet and try to help those fighting and dying. I could only watch as she became smaller and smaller and hordes of Arthro swarmed around her. After I had recovered, I requested her details and wrote to her family several times. Her name was Elaine and I now have her GC portrait in a frame on my desk. She was only nineteen years old.

I have rarely had a peaceful night's sleep since that battle. There was a short period of time where my daughter discovered that I was able to sleep peacefully with her on the sofa in our living room, but since she and my wife had died, I was back to waking in the middle of the night in a cold sweat.

There was a blaring alarm that launched me onto my feet with a start. I tore through the ship's hallways to get to the bridge, finding everyone else there already, except Peter, who appeared out of a service duct a few minutes later.

'What is that?' I yelled, in the moment of silence through the blaring alarm. Naomi fiddled with some buttons on the side and the alarm stopped.

'We found something, a ship. It's spinning through

space,' I looked out the front of the ship. 'We have tried to hail it, but we have not got any response.'

'Another Arthro attack?' I asked.

'Possibly,' Naomi said. 'It's hard to tell, we cannot see any evidence of an attack, no evidence of impact, but it's always possible. It could just be an abandoned ship or it could just be another ambush. Should we check it?'

I thought for a moment.

'Has there been a distress signal broadcast?'

'No, radio silence.' Naomi replied.

'Ok, we can check to see if there are any supplies. The Arthro don't seem smart enough to change tactics this quickly. If the signal before was a trap, they would most likely try it again. I think...I think we will be safe...I hope.'

Everyone except Naomi left the bridge and started to get ready, suiting up in armour and prepping their weapons. I joined them at the lock after a few minutes of getting ready myself. I had just slid my helmet on my head when my earpiece buzzed and I patched it through.

'Yeah?'

'Hey Michael, it's Naomi. You…you should come back to the bridge. There is something that you need to see.'

'Can't it wait? We are just about to board.'

'Michael...right now.' Her voice was serious, so I double-timed it to her.

'Hey kid, what is it?'

She turned to me and pressed a button which closed the door behind me. She stood and cleared her throat, her face white.

'Naomi?' I asked, suddenly concerned, considering her actions. This was unusual behaviour for the usually loud and comedic pilot.

'Michael, please sit. You need to see this, but you need to be sat.' She said, motioning to the chair. I was uneasy, but I complied with her request. I looked at the blank screen in front of me and she tapped in something on the keyboard.

'This ship we found, it's a Cruiser class. I managed to retrieve its base number.' She hesitated before pressing the last button.

The sequence 'XN3827-10GX4' appeared on the screen.

My stomach dropped and I swallowed hard.

'It's the base number of…' I cut her off with a raised hand.

'The ship my family was on.' I said, trying not to be sick. Naomi put her hand on my shoulder.

'Michael, you really don't have to go onto the ship.' I sucked in a deep breath and stood, looking at her, seeing the true concern in her eyes.

'They are dead. I have accepted that fact, it's been two years. I lost them so there is no point in getting my hopes up that they survived this long. We can check the ship for supplies, but we won't find my family.'

'We could at least find their bodies...give them a proper burial.'

I looked at her, softening my expression. I know she was only trying to help.

'We'll scuttle the ship.' I said, 'Then all the dead will be put to rest.'

I started to walk away, leaving Naomi alone on the bridge.

I heard her call after me. 'Your soldiers love you, Michael. You still have a family.'

***

I breathed heavily as I stood in front of the airlock. There was a hiss and the door slid open. In an instant, the room filled with that disgusting smell that we had grown so used to.

'Well, I guess that answers the question of why the ship is spinning through space.' Wallace said.

I ignored him and stepped through the doorway, raising my gun and getting ready to kill anything I saw that had more than four legs. The hallways were dark, lit only by our torches, which wasn't unusual in this situation. Just another obstacle in an already difficult war.

We took our time walking through the dark hallways, finding the door that entered into the food hall, not finding the same horrendous image we found last time. There were no bodies as of yet, making it seem less likely that everyone had been killed by an attack.

'Maybe the crew evacuated before the Arthro arrived?'

Peter said. 'No, wait…'

He pressed a few buttons on the panel on the side of the room and brought up an image with several flashing red dots.

'Only one of the escape shuttles was launched. They can only carry a maximum of fifty people, so there would have been others trapped on the ship.' He explained.

'Sweep the ship.' I said, cutting off Peter. 'This is a salvage mission, not a rescue. If the shuttles didn't launch, it means everyone on board is dead. We can all smell it, there are Arthro on board and we all know, survivors wouldn't be able to last two days, let alone two years. Ignore any bodies you find. Kill any Arthro you come across. They may have moved on from here, but it's unlikely so watch your corners and the ceiling.'

There was a heavy silence before someone spoke.

'Sir…should we look for your…'

'No. Move out.' I said. The group split up and moved away from the food court, beginning to sweep the ship in pairs. The ship had an eerily familiar silence, broken by a faint groan of metal every so often.

Despite almost everyone's protests, I chose to go through the cruiser alone, slowly moving through the hallways, my gun out in front of me. It wasn't long before I heard shouting and gunfire, followed by the shrieking of Arthro. The shrieking stopped quickly and was followed by a buzz on the radio and an 'All clear.' It seemed my wish for small numbers of Arthro had been granted.

I turned a corner, to see a large lump in the corner of the next hallway. As my torchlight passed over it, the lump uncurled and suddenly there was an Arthro scuttling right towards me, shrieking. I backed up quickly and opened fire, hitting it several times in the body and blew off two of its legs. The creature skidded to a stop at my feet but still writhed, so I emptied several more rounds into its body, finally killing it. I sighed and stepped over the body, continuing down the hallway, expecting more of the monsters to come crawling out of the walls. My earpiece suddenly burst into life and made me leap out of my skin.
'Captain, you should probably see this.' The voice said, from Norman. 'Section fifteen.'
I found a map on a nearby wall and planned out my route. I made my way towards the hallway that both Norman and Kim had entered and subsequently called me to.
As I got to the hallway, I came across Norman, who jerked his thumb over his shoulder before he led me on. I followed him through the hallway, up some stairs and entered the secondary deck, which opened up into a long spacious room. There were stairs on the right-hand side, leading up to a long balcony, where there were several more rooms, possibly accommodation. Over by the wall on the left, James and Kim stood, shining their torches on the surface, which was covered

in the brown webbing of the Arthro.

As I approached, I could see the unusual thing they were staring at. Against the wall, held up by the webbing, was a large cocoon-like structure. It was long and thin, about eight by three-foot.

'What the hell is that?'

'No idea, I've never seen one like this before. Usually, their cocoons are about the size of a basketball and in large clusters of thousands,'

'What do we do?' Kim asked.

I thought for a moment.

'Cut it open. Kill whatever is inside.'

Norman seemed to get excited from that suggestion, so he eagerly pulled out his knife. He thrust it into the top of the cocoon and dragged it downwards, a dark brown liquid spewing forth.

A human body slumped out of the cut, already dead. It landed with a sludgy thud.

'My God, what is that?' I exclaimed.

The body was a mix of human and Arthro. The head had started to develop mandibles at the mouth, the arms and legs had fused together and there were several protrusions along the side of the body. From below the neck and all the way down to the ankles, were deep creases going from one side to the other, segmenting the body.

'That looks like…'

'It's a human, turning into an Arthro.' I said with uncertainty.

'Have they been human all this time?' Kim asked, her voice trembling.

'No, there were tests; their biology and DNA are different from humans. This must be new,' James said.

'They must be spinning people up into their cocoons and mutating them.'

'We need to report this back to GC.'

'Kim, get to the Clorha fast, report this back to GC now.' She nodded and ran.

'God, how many of the human Arthro have we killed?' Norman asked, his voice starting to break.

'There have never been any reports of anything like this before. This must be an isolated incident,' I said. 'We should burn this place.' I went to reach for my grenades.

'Sir, surely we should finish the sweep of the ship before we do that? It is our duty to ensure there are no survivors.' James said.

'Look around you. This ship is silent. There are no survivors. Everyone is dead and it is our duty to prevent the spread of whatever this is.' I said, gesturing to the mutated body.

I tapped my communicator and I heard it click into the joint frequency.

'This is Captain Lewes. I am giving a direct order; all persons are to immediately return to the Clorha. I shall be detonating a combustion grenade in five minutes. Out.' I clicked my communicator off and gestured for James and Norman to leave.

I waited next to the husk, the five minutes passing in relative silence. I took one of the grenades off my belt and pulled the pin, holding onto the safety lever. I clicked my communicator on again and ordered a roll call.

Everyone confirmed they were back on the Clorha, so I turned and threw the grenade at the furthest corner.

The moment it left my hand, I was running, making my way down to the first deck and towards the airlock. As I reached the bottom of the stairs, I heard the grenade detonate and the fire roar as it engulfed the room.

As I turned the final corner that would lead to the Clorha, several Arthro blocked off my escape. In an instant, I pulled my rifle off my shoulder and fired towards them, hitting them as they darted towards me with a screech.

None of them reached me, my bullets tearing through their fleshy bodies and severing several of their legs and mandibles. I could feel the heat of the fire begin to grow in intensity from behind me, indicating my time to leave. I carefully stepped between the corpses of the monsters, on guard in case any were simply playing possum.

As I stepped over the final Arthro, my eyes caught a small glimpse of something sticking out of the flesh, just below the creature's head. I bent down and looked at it closely, seeing it was a piece of shiny metal. The intensity of the heat was high, but I had a few minutes

before the fire reached the hallway.
I pulled out my knife and cut into the flesh, prising out the thing.
It was a thin, flat piece of metal, slightly rusted where it had been exposed to the air and part of the edge had been dented by a bullet. I wiped the brown blood off the piece and looked at it closely.
It was half a heart, with the word 'Michael.'

Naomi's voice crackled through the earpiece but I almost didn't hear it as I stared at the piece of metal.
'Micha…can you hea….are…there?....my Go…. What is th….What the fu…oh my…Mic….'
I slowly rose to my feet and looked around the dark, empty corridor, swimming in my own mind. I vomited, the liquid running down my helmet and into my suit, which whirred as it processed it.
The voices in my ear continued.
'Michael…Plea…respond….I'm scared….what is it? Can you see it? We nee…leave.'
Behind Naomi's voice on the communicator, I could hear voices, screaming, crying and praying. The voices of my crew.
I walked towards the closest window and looked out into the eternity of space.
There, I saw it.
An entity. A cosmic being. A God of the universe. Pulsing and writhing as its surface teemed with Arthro. The home of the enemy was a being, not a planet.

A billion miles wide, slowly moving through the eternity of space, floating, propelled by fins that slowly bristled and flexed.
If I had a thousand days to describe it, not even the greatest minds could understand what it looked like.
I stared at its eyes. Oh god, its eyes. They stared back and tore through my soul, making my nose bleed.
I looked at the half of the metal heart in my hand, and then I stared at the God of the universe.
A tear ran down my face.
The intensity of the heat from the combustion grenade grew from behind. I closed my eyes and welcomed the burning embrace.

Beware the Fae

Joe sat on the floor with a small thump, his bag still on his back. With a sigh, he pulled it off and placed it between his legs. Opening it, he plunged both of his hands in and started to rummage.
'Anything good?' I asked, edging forward slightly.
He exhaled and pulled out a small red box.
'It's a bit poor taste, considering.' He said, tossing it to me.
I caught the box in the air between us and looked at it. Lucky Charms cereal. A huge green leprechaun stared right at me. I stifled a laugh and opened the box, pulling out the inner packaging and folding up the box and placing it on the fire. I ate about half of the dry cereal and little marshmallows, before passing it back to Joe. He too ate them with an expression of slight ambivalence.
We kicked out the small fire and picked up our bags. I picked up my hunting rifle and slung it over my shoulder, the stock hitting the back of my knee and adding to the already purple bruise that was there. We started down the small dirt path that led to the main road, scattered with empty abandoned cars and we took our time to slowly move through them, avoiding tossed luggage and some corpses. Most of the bodies had started to decay, remnants from the Revelation and the mass hysteria that followed.

We walked along the road for a few miles, before we encountered a collapsed bridge. There were several cars at the bottom of the small gully, some of which had corpses within, splayed out of the windows and broken on the grassy floor.

At this time, without any witnesses, there is no way of determining what exactly caused the collapse but there wasn't any real point in dwelling on it.

'Laura, over here.' I heard Joe call.

We made our way down a steep embankment, slipping and cursing until we got to the bottom.

'Ready for the climb back up?' Joe said, nudging me with his arm.

'Maybe you can climb up first and throw me down a rope.' I said.

'Nah, can't. Your arse is too fat.' He cackled like a hyena and ran away before I could tell him to shut up. Sometimes I really hated him.

The other side of the gully wasn't as steep as the previous, so we slowly clambered up, at times walking on two feet and others, on all fours, our hands gripping onto the grass.

Joe got to the top first and looked around, keeping somewhat low.

'All clear.' He said, turning back to face me. He held onto a small tree with his left hand and reached his right hand out for me to take.

I breathed deeply and reached out for his hand and I missed it, slipping slightly, pulling my hand back to grip the grass and stop my sudden descent. I started to climb again, looking up towards Joe. I reached my hand out and grabbed his, his fingers curling around my hand tightly.

I froze.

'Laura? What…?'

'Don't move.' I hissed.

Joe stayed as still as he could, as the sound of fluttering grew louder. He did his best to control his breathing and stay as quiet as possible. It was too late.

They had seen us.

The fluttering grew louder. It was a soft noise, quickly followed by child-like giggling.

I saw two tiny hands appear over Joe's left shoulder, followed by a small dandelion shaped head. Under a bright yellow flower head, appeared a small green face, with simple, yet cute, features. It had small black eyes, a button nose and a little mouth. Pointed ears sat either side of the head, which twitched slightly.

The small figure pulled themselves completely up to stand on Joe's shoulder, their clothing was made of dandelion leaves and they had small butterfly wings on their back. They giggled quietly as they studied his face, their hands gently reaching out and caressing his cheek.

I stared at Joe's face; his face was painted with fear. He swallowed hard.

'Run.' He said. With that, he threw my hand back and the momentum pulled me backwards. I fell for what seemed like an age, towards the grass below me. As I fell and skidded down the verge, thorns tore at my skin and my hands hit stinging nettles. My vision stayed on Joe until he was suddenly pulled backwards violently and he started yelling and grunting. It soon turned into screaming and there was an animalistic roar.

I stopped when I reached the bottom of the gully and landed hard on my back, my rifle falling off my shoulder. I was immediately on my feet and I grabbed the gun. I stared up towards the top of the incline, doing everything I could to not call out for Joe. His screaming had stopped by the time I was back on my feet but the animalistic growling and roaring had not. There was movement at the top of the incline and I started to back up. There was a loud crack of breaking branches as something leapt into the air and a loud boom as it landed right in front of me.

The faun pulled itself up to full height, towering over me by a good two feet, maybe more. It snorted and huffed, dark and wet blood covering its hands and mouth.

I slowly stepped back, keeping my eyes fixed on it. The faun stomped its left hoof and hunched slightly, getting ready.

In a flash of movement, it kicked up dirt and charged forward and, in a reactionary move, I raised my rifle and fired a single shot without aiming, barely getting the stock against my shoulder.

The sudden gunshot made my ears ring.

The bullet grazed the skull of the faun, splitting its skin and small amounts of blood splashed onto the green grass.

The faun bellowed and reared, its hands covering the wound as it fell backwards. I instantly turned and sprinted towards a row of trees further along the gully. It was risky to enter a forest, but I had to get out of the open.

l weaved myself between the trees, getting deeper and deeper into the woodland, hoping to have lost the faun.

I hid against a large oak tree for a couple of hours, listening and waiting, ensuring I had not been followed. I cursed as I realised the sun was low and would soon set so I moved away from the tree in order to find a way out of the forest.

Being in a forest was dangerous enough, even more so at night.

I walked through the forest carefully, but my slow pace meant that it was soon dusk. Night followed quickly and I was eventually forced to use the light from the moon that broke through the trees.

The deathly silence of the forest was broken by the sound of light and sweet giggling. I slung my rifle over my back and pulled out my knife, moving low to the ground, slowly and quietly. The giggling echoed around the forest, fading and growing in volume. I saw several small lights zip back and forth, stopping together a few times, before zipping off again.

There was a giggle right next to my ear and I flinched, flailing my hand at the rose petal pixie, which darted away from my hand, their giggle turning into a snarl. I grabbed for them, but they avoided my hand and slashed at me with tiny thorns.

The pixie darted several feet away and I launched myself in their direction, my free hand grabbing for them. I missed again but dropped my knife in order to grab them with my right hand as they moved away from my left. This move caught them by surprise and my hand wrapped around the waist of the pixie. Several thorns punctured the skin of my hand but I ignored the pain, holding the squirming pixie tightly.

The pixie started to scream, so I quickly picked up my knife and plunged it into their tiny chest.

They squealed and thrashed at my hand before going limp and I watched as the body turned grey and scattered into loose ash in my palm, which I quickly dusted off using my other hand.

I looked around, to see the other pixies flying in the opposite direction.

They hadn't heard anything.

I slowly backed away, not turning until I had lost sight of them in the cold and dark forest.

***

'Don't move or I'll blast your head off.'

The old man held the shotgun pointed towards me, rested on his hip. I held my hands up in my best attempt at looking harmless.

'I'm not a threat. I just need to sit and rest, if I may.' I said.

Sat around the fire that the old man guarded, were two other women, a young girl and a boy.

'Lose the rifle.' The old man said, using his shotgun to gesture. Using my left hand, I gently took my rifle off my right shoulder and held it by the strap.

'It's empty. I only had one bullet and I used it.' I said, holding it out towards the group, like an offering to an ancient god.

The young girl looked at the old man and he nodded firmly. She stood and took it from me, pulling the bolt back and peering inside the chamber. She closed the bolt and passed the gun back to me, stock first. I shook my head and she shrugged in acceptance, passing it to one of the women. The old man lowered his gun but he kept his eyes on me.

'Come, sit.' The young girl said. 'My name is Emily.'

'Laura.' I said, as I sat down next to the fire.

Pointing around the fire, the girl continued.

'That's Grampa Earl, Grandma Ruth, Gina and Artie.'

I gently waved at each of them. Ruth passed me a small cup and I was ecstatic to discover it was tea. I took a huge gulp, burning my tongue and throat.

The camp was small, consisting of a small fire surrounded by several wooden logs acting like seats. There was a 4x4 car, with a trailer and a large plastic barrel, full of water. There were several sleeping bags between the logs and fire and what looked like a rolled-up tarp. Just next to the fire, was a bowl of steaming broth. with hot coals underneath.

'How old are you dear?' Grandma Ruth asked, looking at my face, trying to see past the dirt and blood.

I wiped my mouth and said, 'Twenty three. I think. The days have blurred into one so often I feel like I've lost more time than I realise.'

'Are you alone?'

'Uh…' I swallow. 'Yes. I was with my brother, but he was taken. He is probably dead now.'

The words hit me like a punch as I said them, the reality of my past day coming at me in full swing as the last of my adrenaline drained away.

'We are sorry to hear that dear.' The old woman placed her hand on my knee and I found my hand taking hers and squeezing it. The sudden affection broke the barriers and I started to sob, the elderly woman pulling me into a tight embrace as I mourned Joe. Grandma Ruth was warm and kind. I missed my own Grandmother.

Gina passed me a small plastic plate of steaming broth and I started to eat. I think there was rabbit in it and it tasted good. I ate it too quickly. My stomach would probably take its revenge on me later.

'Where did you lose your brother?' Grandpa Earl asked. Grandma Ruth shot him a stern look, but he simply shrugged.

'Don't answer that.' She said. 'He is paranoid that the

fae may have followed you, but we are safe here. The iron keeps them away.'

'Alright, fine.' Grandpa Earl said. Instead, he pointed at the rifle I had given to the young girl, which was now leaning against a small pile of logs.

'Are you any good with that?'

'No.' I said bluntly. 'I've only ever had two bullets and I missed with the first. The other barely hit the target. That thing is useless to me. You should keep it.'

'Useless without bullets.' Grandpa Earl said, spitting into the fire. It fizzed and Artie clapped excitedly.

We sat and ate and drank in silence for a few moments.

'What did you do before the Revelation?' Emily asked.

'I had just started Year Eight at OakGrange school.'

'I was going into Year Six!' Artie declared loudly and Grandma Ruth shushed him gently.

'I had finished a business course at university and had been working at my dad's company. He ran a delivery and shipping firm and I was helping him out with some accounts and admin.' I said, 'I had been working there for about a year before the Revelation happened.'

'What happened to your parents?' Emily asked, her hand taking mine.

'They died. Or, I think they did. I haven't seen them since. It was just myself and my brother Joe. Now it's just me.'

'Fucking fairies.' Grandpa Earl snarled.

'Earl, language!' That was Grandma Ruth. She slapped his knee and he went quiet. I sat in silence for a moment.

'I used to love fairies and fables. I particularly loved stories about witches. I used to make my mother read me 'Hansel and Gretel' every night before I went to sleep. Even after she did that, I would stay up at night and read it again under the covers.' I laughed slightly. 'The first time I ever encountered a witch; I ended up driving a rusted iron pole through her gut.'

The rest of the group stayed silent. I suddenly had a wave of embarrassment flush over me. I had been talking too much.

'I'm so sorry. I've been very self-focused. How did you all get here?'

Grandma Ruth laughed and patted my hand.

'It's alright dear. Earl and I are married and were retired in a small cottage. Artie and Emily are our grandchildren. They were visiting us when the Revelation happened.' She dropped her voice to a whisper. 'We don't know where their parents are anymore.'

I realised she had done that for the sake of Artie, who was now watching Grandpa Earl poke the fire with a long stick.

'We met Gina on the road and invited her to join us.'

'I was a biochemist.' Gina said, speaking for the first time. Her voice was a lot deeper than I imagined it would be and she spoke with the slightest of lisps. 'Before all of this crap, if you had told me that fairies and magical creatures were real, I would have probably either laughed you out of the room or arrogantly proved to you how they were not. I was rather involved in my work, but it was my passion.' She drank from her cup, making a face at the now stone cold tea.

'When my girlfriend showed me the news of the Revelation, I laughed and thought it was a prank or a late April Fool's joke. I left my house like any other day to go to work. The bus I was on was hit by a centaur stampede and I barely managed to get off the road as they crushed cars and people. I ran all the way home, only to find my front door smashed down.'

I sat in silence. I was worried that it would be rude to ask to know what had happened.

Gina continued without prompt.

'I found Alice in the living room. Her body had been crushed and folded up, stuffed into a corner of the room. Her body was no larger than a shoebox. There was this tall skeletal creature sitting in the opposite corner. Its fingers were just as long as its arms. It muttered the word "Baubas" several times before it went for me. I screamed and ran and left Alice to rot in that corner.'

She had started to cry and Emily went and hugged her. Grandma Ruth passed her another cup of steaming tea.

'I've not seen one of those.' I said. 'It sounds horrible. I'm sorry.'

There was a sudden howling across the night sky and we all flinched. Instinctively I had drawn my knife. The howling died down after a moment or so and

Grandpa Earl stood. He picked up his shotgun.
'I'm going to go check the perimeter.'
With that, he disappeared into the darkness that surrounded the fire.
Artie looked worried so Gina sat on the floor with him and they gently conversed.
'That sounded like Black Shuck.' He said, his voice trembling.
'It did.' Gina said, 'But as Grandpa Earl just said, we have the iron fences. We will be safe. They can't get to us here.'
Artie nodded and seemed to calm down. Grandpa Earl was gone a few minutes and eventually came back, stepping into the circle of light from the fire.
'All secure'. He said.
'Then,' Grandma Ruth said, 'I suggest we get some sleep. Gina, will you take the first watch, followed by Earl?' Gina nodded.
Grandma Ruth turned to me. 'Laura my dear, would you be so kind as to take a watch?'
'Of course.' I said. 'I can take the second watch. Grandpa Earl, you look like you need some sleep.'
Grandpa Earl nodded and thanked me.

I stared up at the night sky, enjoying the sheer number of stars that were visible. They blanketed the deep black of space, constellations dancing and churning together in a mass of glitter that often felt blinding. The moon hung in the air, acting as their guardian, lighting the night up even brighter.

Joe believed the fae had started the Revelation in order to try and stop humans from hurting the Earth. While I don't know if his theory was right, I had to admit, the fae had seemed to make the atmosphere cleaner. I closed my eyes and fell into a dreamless sleep, my final thought being of Joe. Gina woke me up after a few hours and I took my watch. I sat and watched the fire, pulling out my book and reading a few pages. I had never been a fan of Shakespeare before the Revelation but Twelfth Night was all I had and frankly, I had been enjoying it a lot more than I thought I would. After a short while, Grandpa Earl stirred and awoke, getting up and picking up his shotgun.

'Go on.' He said, 'Back to sleep.'

I thanked him and lay down again.

I examined the fence that I had avoided seeing most of in the dark of the previous night. There were four Iron chains, parallel to each other, linking between dozens of iron rods, encircling the camp.

'These must have been hard to find.' I said, amazed at the sheer volume of iron.

'We found a scrap heap and frankly, these were a god damn phenomenon. We managed to use a couple of carts and trolleys and get them here and make this small encampment. It's quite useful to have a secure basecamp.'

'I can imagine.' I said. 'I hated sleeping in the open. I was always scared I would awaken to a wendigo eating my guts.'

'You said you killed a witch.' Grandpa Earl said. 'Any more than that?'

'A few.' I said. 'A couple of pixies and a monopod.'

'You're shitting me. Really? You?' Grandpa Earl said with no attempt to hide his disbelief.

'Well, me and Joe. Joe tackled it from behind and I drove my knife into its skull.'

'Well, damn. That's one hell of a kill. I've seen those things take down a van.' Grandpa Earl said, rubbing his hands together vigorously, driving off the cold.

'What about you?' I asked. 'What was your first kill?'

Grandpa Earl went silent. He looked around, making sure we were alone.

'Don't tell Ruth.'

I crossed my heart in a gesture.

'It was just after the Revelation and the death of my Son and his wife. I was full of anger and I wanted to kill a fae. I don't know how my son died, but I knew that those monsters had brutalised them. Made them suffer.' He took a deep breath.

'I left in the early morning, before light. I walked for an hour before I saw any fae but I finally found one. I found a single Blemmey, sat alone against a tree, sleeping. I had bought a bag along with me, full of rope, which I used to tie it up before it woke.'

'What did you do after that?' I asked, taking a step towards the old man.

'I sat in front of it and waited for it to wake up. When it

did, I started to pray. I prayed to God for the power to help me do what I needed to.' He looked down at his hands and saw they were trembling. He clasped them together softly and took several deep breaths.

'Do you know that fae experience fear? Because they do. I saw it in the creature's eyes. Those large, bulbous eyes in its chest glistened with tears and it started panting. It was terrified of me. But I didn't stop. I was angry and it was going to die.'

I gently took his hand in mine, fearful of him suddenly floating away.

'I made it suffer. I made it cry and beg and retch and bleed. I was more of a monster that day than it was.' He said, his voice scarily calm.

I squeezed his hand tightly. I didn't know what to say.

'Please, don't tell Ruth.' He said softly.

'I won't.' I said, with no intention of that being a lie.

***

My eyes bolted open to the sound of crashing iron, blood-curdling screams and thundering hooves. Quickly wiping the sleep from my eyes, I looked around the camp, the early light of morning coated with a thin film of mist. I could see dozens of shapes speeding past, large silhouettes encircling the camp. A hand grabbed my shoulder and I spun around, coming face to face with Grandma Ruth. Blood streaked down her face.

'They broke through the fence. Get out of here girl.

Run.'

'But…where…' I started as I looked around, trying to see through the mist. It cleared for a moment and I could see the now slack iron fence, most of which was lying on the ground. On the other side, dozens of centaurs galloped around the perimeter, whooping and hollering still unable to cross over the now slack iron chain. One suddenly rocketed past me and Grandma Ruth and we scrambled out of the way.

'There is a small gap in the fence.' Grandma Ruth said, looking around. 'Laura, get away from here. Try and find Emily. She managed to run before this all started.'

'But…what about…' The old woman grabbed me by the arms so hard it hurt.

'Artie and Gina are dead. I don't know where Earl is but he can handle himself. Please.' I nodded as my mouth had gone dry.

'There is a forest that way. Make a break for the trees.' Grandma Ruth said, pointing towards the rising sun. There was a gunshot. All the encircling shapes suddenly stopped and charged in one direction, creating an opening.

'Now run!' She bellowed.

She moved before I could, running into the centre of the camp and picked up a pan and a cup. She clanged them together and started to yell. There was a rumbling of hooves towards her and large horse bodies appeared out of the mist. Huge human hands grabbed Grandma Ruth tightly around the arms and she struggled against them as the centaur slowly lifted her up to face them. I covered my mouth to stop myself from crying out as a horse's mouth engulfed her head, a loud and solid crunch following immediately after. Grandma Ruth screamed as she died.

'Fuck!' I shouted as I bolted towards the sun, hoping I could outrun a momentarily distracted horse creature. I leapt over the iron chain, now nothing more than a line snaking through the grass. The pounding hooves stopped momentarily as the centaur was unable to pass over the iron, giving me a chance. I ran and ran as the sound of galloping hooves grew louder as the creatures outside of the iron ring descended on me. I was helpless. Helpless and small.

There was a loud 'boom!'

I looked over my shoulder to see the centaurs had stopped, looking back to the flames licking up from the centre of the camp, originating from the car. I took the opportunity the explosion gave and continued to run. A single centaur never looked at the explosion, instead, it kept its attention to me, its black eyes and ears staying forward. It bared its teeth with a whinny.

I reached the edge of the forest, vaulting a fallen tree, barrelling around a few others and then ducked into some thickets, hoping to lose the creature. I hugged the dirt, pulling leaves and dirt around me, to mask my scent and for visual camouflage.

The centaur slowly walked through the forest, its head raised, large horse nostrils sniffing the air in loud puffs.

Its hands were large and calloused, attached to arms of pure muscle. Its chest featured an almost comic-like six-pack, which stopped just above the belly button. Beneath that, was the brown body of a shire horse. I hated centaurs. I wished they had human heads instead of horse ones. There was something unsettling about a horse head on a human body.

The centaur stopped in its tracks, sniffing the air again. Its ears twitched and suddenly, its fists clenched and were raised. The centaur turned its head to the left and there was a shot.

Buckshot tore through its muzzle, stripping flesh, muscle and blood off of bone. The centaur bellowed and reared up as another shot rang out, this one hitting it in the side and causing it to fall. It landed on its side a few inches away from me, writhing and bellowing. Grandpa Earl ran towards it, pulling out a rusted hatchet, which he buried in the skull of the centaur. The horse limbs thrashed for a moment before Grandpa Earl struck it a second time and it stopped.

I sighed a breath of relief and stood slowly.

He saw the movement and raised his weapon, sighing with relief and lowering it once he saw it was me.

'Laura. Thank god.'

'Earl…' I started.

'I know. I know Ruth is gone. As is Artie and Gina. Not Emily though. She must be in the forest somewhere.' He looked down at the centaur and sighed. 'The fence didn't break, you know.' He said, not

looking up as he loaded his shotgun. 'Someone unlinked it. They made a gap and the fae got inside.'
'Earl…' I said again, my voice breaking.
He looked up to me with a 'huh?' before slowly turning.
A figure rose above him, long limbs extending to its full height. It towered a good few feet over Grandpa Earl who looked up at the figure.
A long grey and brown beard hung from the filthy mouth, covering the grey skin of the broad body, which was impossibly held up by two long, bird-like legs. On the feet were two clunky and rough sets of iron boots. The feet hissed with heat and I could smell the burning flesh, which made me gag.
The arms of the creature were just as thin as the legs, though they ended in large, wide palmed hands. Most of the head, except the mouth, which was full of rotten teeth, was covered by a cap of deeply stained red.
Before I could say anything, the creature raised the broken wooden pole it held and thrust it into the chest of Grandpa Earl. I yelped in shock.
Grandpa Earl gurgled for a moment and spat blood, raising his gun and managed to fire it into the face of the Redcap. It bellowed as its hands covered its face and it crashed into a tree. Grandpa Earl fell to his knees and slumped to his side.
I turned and ran deeper into the forest.
I ran through the trees, carefully checking the ground I stepped on, avoiding any mushrooms I saw.

I slowed when I saw a shadow move in a small clearing in front of me. I pressed against the oak tree closest to me and carefully peered around it. Sat at the edge of the clearing, furiously rubbing two sticks together was Emily. My stomach dropped and I raced forward, keeping my head low and checking over my shoulder. She looked towards the sudden movement, her eyes wide with horror and then as she saw me, surprise.

'Laura!' She almost screamed, running forwards and throwing her arms around me, before breaking down in loud and heavy sobs.

'How did you get away?' Emily asked. 'The last I saw, the camp was surrounded.'

'It was all Grandpa Earl. He set off an explosion which distracted the fae. I was able to get away.' I paused. 'He is dead. They all are.'

Emily slowly nodded. She returned to her sticks, rubbing them together, trying to start a fire.

'Grandma Ruth said you managed to get away before all of this happened?' I asked, looking at the young girl. 'Why were you awake so early?'

'Hmm? Oh, I couldn't sleep so I decided to have a small walk around the camp.' She said, not looking away from the sticks.

'Then, did you see what happened to the fence? Why did it fall?' I asked, hopeful for some insight.

Emily answered without looking at me.

'Oh, because I knocked it over.'

My heart stopped for a second and my stomach lurched.

I sat in silence and stared at the young girl who rubbed and rubbed the sticks until they smouldered and she placed them under some dry grass. She squealed with delight as small flames licked at the sticks she started to place on top.

'What?' I managed to utter.

'I walked to the iron fence, knocked over one of the supports and let the fae into the camp.' Emily said, like a student explaining how they worked out a maths equation. She rubbed her hands together and held them over the small fire she had just made.

I attempted to process my thoughts, but before I could say anything, Emily spoke again.

'I suppose you want to know why?' She still didn't look at me.

'Yes.' I said, bluntly.

She turned her head and stared at me for a moment.

'You really can't tell, can you? Wow, humans are stupid.'

She cleared her throat and spoke as though she was explaining to a three-year-old.

'I'm fae.'

I shook my head violently.

'No, you can't be. You've touched iron. I've seen it.'

'Changelings are resistant to iron. Not much point in having a sleeper agent if they can be given away by something that is used almost everywhere.' Emily said.

'You…you are a changeling?' I said, my hands fumbling for my knife.

'Don't bother. I just said the iron won't hurt me.' Emily said.

'I can still cut off your head.' I said, swallowing hard so as to not vomit.

'You could.' Emily said, pointing away. 'But then, who would ensure that they killed you quickly?'

I looked up to follow the direction that Emily pointed towards.

Several cyclops' stumbled out of the forest, their long arms dragging along the ground. The cyclops' walked with their mouths opening and closing like fish, with their lazy eye wandering back and forth. This was made even more unsettling by the fact their mouths and eyes were switched in place. There was more movement and a cyclops appeared behind me.

'I really did like you Laura. Really, I did.' Emily said. 'You were one of the nicer humans.'

The Ones that Crawl Out are Fat and Stout

My eyes opened slowly to darkness. I tried to stretch, but my arms bumped against something solid, stopping them close to my side. I tried to pull my legs up, but the same thing happened and my knees hit something above me. I turned my head as much as I could, only to find I had limited movement all around.
I felt around myself as much as I could, my fingers feeling along the wooden side and top of the thing I was lying in. I started to sweat as I realised, with fear, that I was in a makeshift wooden box.
I started to scream, banging with fists against the top of the box, my cries being lost to the darkness.

I must have passed out as I found my eyes opening again to the same darkness, with no recollection of how long it had been since I had first awoken. I struggled, pushing against the top of the box with all the strength I could muster in my arms, but the wooden lid held firm.
I went to scream and shout again, but as I opened my mouth, I heard muffled voices.
'Is this the one?' Said the first voice.
'Yeah, I'm sure of it. I saw them bury it earlier today.' Said the second.
'Let's get started. The sooner we start digging the

better.' Said the first.

I stayed absolutely still, lying in the silent darkness, listening for the sound of digging, hoping that this was to be my salvation.

After a few minutes, I couldn't hear anything, so I started yelling and banging against the lid again, hoping the voices outside would hear and dig faster. There were no more voices.

Using my fingers, I carefully felt around the sides and edges of the box, trying to visualise it through the darkness. The edges and corners were flush and the wood had been sanded to a smooth finish. Whoever made this box did it very well. Time and effort and care had been put into making this. Maybe I should be thankful at least that I wouldn't get a splinter.

I tried to push the lid off again, using both my arms and knees, but it still didn't budge. It was getting harder and harder to breathe, so I did what I could to keep my breathing steady and low. I heard the voices again.

'How far down did they bury him?' said the first.

'Quite far it seems.' said the second. 'Guess they really didn't want anyone to find him here. Unusual for someone to be buried in a forest and not a graveyard.'

A forest? Why the hell was I buried in a forest? All I remember from the previous night was going to bed, but now I'm buried alive.

I screamed. I banged the lid and sides of the box. I kicked and struggled and thrashed. I shouted for help until my throat was raw and I sobbed for someone to save me.

My eyes opened slowly, not to the light of day, but the same darkness from before. I could barely move. I could barely breathe, my body taking in nothing more than short and shallow gasps. I struggled to keep my eyes open as my time was rapidly running out.

'Here we are.' said the second voice.

'Ah, yes, you were right!' said the first voice.

'Help me…' I croaked, awaiting the breaking and splintering of wood above me and for oxygen to flood my lungs.

Something long and thin hit my face with a wet slap. A second thing followed with the same wet slap. I tried to reach up to touch them, but my arms wouldn't listen to my brain and remained slack at my sides. My eyes started to close and I fought to keep them half-open.

'Oh, it's still alive!' said the first worm.

'What luck, nothing quite like fresh food if you ask me. Start with the eyes. They are better warm.' said the second.

The Tree

<u>Friday, 10th March 2017</u>
School was alright. I can't believe that Johnson gave us a thousand-word essay as homework. Just how I wanted to spend my weekend, staring at a piece of paper and writing about a poem which frankly, I think is a piece of crap.
Oh, also, to make things worse…I scratched my head on a twig hanging from a tree today. I hate my life.

<u>Wednesday 5th April 2017</u>
Just watched the series finale of Space Cadets. Not as dramatic and mind-bending as I had hoped, but it was alright. Probably going to discuss it with Sam tomorrow. School was ok.
That stick hit my head again. Tried to pull it down but it was a bit too bendy to break. Might take some scissors along tomorrow.

<u>Saturday 20th May 2017</u>
Had lunch with Sam today. The bastard told me he was going to pay for it, but he claimed to have 'forgotten his wallet' so I had to pay.
He said he would get the next one. I don't believe him.

That stick was there again. It seemed to have grown back after I cut it down. If anything, it seemed longer.

Saturday, 10th June 2017
I swear, I swear, that tree attacked me. I can't explain it, other than the branch seemed to just swing at me. My parents don't believe me, but I'm sure it happened. It wasn't the wind. The branch actively swung at me.
I'm going to have Sam walk with me tomorrow, so he can see it too.

Sunday, 11th June 2017
Sam came along with me. He kept joking that the tree was trying to 'feel me up' and was going to stalk me home. He wouldn't stop, even when we got to the tree. Of course, nothing happened.
I hate my life.

Thursday 13th July 2017
Sam was right. The tree…it followed me home. I can hear it, tapping on the window.

It keeps calling my name…

Printed in Great Britain
by Amazon